DATE DUE

FIC
GRI

Griffiths, Helen
The greyhound

474

The Greyhound

The Greyhound

Every day, no matter what the weather, Jamie waited to see the old man and his dog. It was an old, sad, thin greyhound—but to Jamie that dog gave his life meaning, and was his dream.

Finally, the day came when Jamie could call Silver his own, and on that day Jamie's time of heartache and fear began. Silver was all the boy had hoped he would be—a wonderful, loving companion—but Jamie had to hide him and feed him, and those two problems created troubles almost beyond the endurance of a boy of eleven.

Author Helen Griffiths takes us into postwar London: the crowded apartment where Jamie's family struggles along, the noisy market stalls of Club Row, the deserted bombed site where Jamie and Silver hide out, the local school where the young delinquents get Jamie into their power and almost destroy him.

The characters—Jamie, shy and impractical, his harassed mother, his resourceful sister, his swaggering enemies, and, above all, Silver the greyhound—are drawn with the same drama and subtlety which made Miss Griffiths' book, *The Wild Heart*, so compelling.

By the Same Author

THE WILD HEART

The Greyhound

HELEN GRIFFITHS

Illustrated by Victor G. Ambrus

DOUBLEDAY & COMPANY, INC., GARDEN CITY, NEW YORK

474

Contents

Glossary

British money	*Approximate* *American equivalent*
1 pence (in slang, a "tanner" is sixpence)	1 cent
1 shilling (a "bob" in slang)	14 cents
a half crown	35 cents
1 pound (a "quid" in slang)	$2.80
1 guinea	$2.94

1

The White Greyhound

I

It was a dull, early spring day in London. The pavements were damp from the rain of the previous night and trickles of water seeped along the gutters. A playful breeze brushed showers of clinging drops from the new green leaves of the plane trees in the square, while far above them and the gaunt, gray buildings was a gloomy, cloud-streaked sky, heavy with the promise of more rain.

At the edge of the pavement, opposite the square, stood a boy. One hand was in a trouser pocket and the other pressed close against his side as, sunk into utter boredom, he concentrated solely on an empty cigarette packet lying soggy in the gutter, pushing it back and forth with the toe of his shoe.

He was not very tall. He was thin, eleven years old, with straight fair hair falling untidily over his forehead and gray eyes. He was wearing a red pullover and a green shirt but neither was thick enough to keep him warm.

It was a Saturday morning and he had nothing to do. His mother had an early job on Saturdays and his father was probably still asleep in bed, having worked a late shift on the buses the previous night. His sister Cora was at home looking after the baby and Jamie had escaped from the house as quickly as he could, just in case she tried to nag him into washing up the breakfast dishes or doing some shopping. He usually went to the pictures on Saturday morning but he had only fivepence halfpenny in his pockets. Not enough.

So Jamie just stood there, feeling cold and forlorn, thinking of the third episode of "Superman" which he was going to miss, and kicking at the cigarette packet because he had nothing else to do.

He stopped to gaze at the man who was coming up the street.

He was old and bent, with a pronounced limp and a greyhound on a piece of string trotting sedately at his side. The man wore a shabby black coat which was far too long, reaching almost to his ankles. His throat and half his head were muffled in a long tasselled scarf, so aged that its original color was indistinguishable. Jamie soon lost interest in him. He saw him nearly every

morning, always wearing the same coat and scarf. Jamie transferred an admiring gaze upon the dog.

It was much taller than his baby sister, with long, delicately shaped legs and a thin, ropy sort of tail which clung to its hindquarters as if glued there. Even when he wagged it, which was seldom, only the tip wavered, slightly and uncertainly. He was mostly white, a rather dirty white, with hair rubbed up the wrong way, and he had one black ear and one brown one. His eyes were narrow and dull, a sort of yellow color, and he never took any notice of the boy who clicked his tongue or snapped his fingers to attract his attention. He was a very disdainful dog.

His master took him to the square almost every day for exercise. He never spoke to the dog, unless it was to call him to heel or to order him to sit, and he never spoke to Jamie, although he saw him often and could not fail to notice the interest he took in the dog.

He came up to where Jamie was standing and, with back turned to him, waited to cross the road. The dog looked bored and not at all eager to reach the square and Jamie felt sorry for him. He thought it must be awful for a dog to go exactly the same way every day, for exactly the same number of minutes, and not be allowed to pause to sniff the paving stones and lampposts as other dogs did.

Suddenly he asked, "What's his name, mister?"

"Eh! What did you say?"

The old man turned slowly to stare at Jamie with petulant eyes. Jamie grinned.

"What's his name—the dog's name?" he repeated.

"Silver, I call him, but that's not what's written on his pedigree."

"Gosh!" exclaimed Jamie. "Has he got a pedigree?"

"Every greyhound that can be called a greyhound's got a pedigree. His real name's Silver Streak by Lightning out of Flying Exit."

"Gosh!" said Jamie again, and before he could say any more the old man left the pavement and hurried across to the square, fumbling in his pocket for the key.

The dog did not look back but followed at his usual pace, with his dry, black nose pressed against the old man's leg, the string hanging loosely from his collar.

Jamie waited until they were safely in the square before following them. A greyhound with a name like that must be really important. Perhaps the old man was training him for the race track or keeping him in good condition for the Greyhound Derby. He did not know much about the Greyhound Derby except that last year his father had bet two shillings each way on a dog and lost, but, nevertheless, Jamie decided to watch. After all, he could do no harm and, as the man did not seem to mind answering his questions, he ought not to mind having a spectator.

He stood with his hands in his pockets and his head pressed against the rusty railings while raindrops dripped down his neck, wishing that he could be inside the square with the old man instead of having to stand where he was. His view was partially blocked by a clump of sooty rhododendrons and smoky-colored tree trunks and it was only occasionally that he caught a glimpse of the fabulous Silver Streak by Lightning out of Flying

Exit. What a name! It made his own, James Vincent, sound rather inadequate.

Too soon the ten minutes were up and Jamie had seen little but the greyhound's ropy tail quavering halfheartedly or his white body shivering with cold. He was too far away to catch up with the old man and his dog when they left the square, but he did not mind. He would not have known what to say if he had done so.

He watched the greyhound's movements with a surge of pride and affection. Fancy knowing a dog with a name like that!

II

From then on Jamie thought a lot about the greyhound. Although he had seen him often before and admired him only distantly, the fact that he now knew the dog's name made a great deal of difference. He developed a personal interest in him, wishing that he had not wasted so much time before, and eagerly looked forward to seeing the old man every day so that he could ask him more questions and perhaps even venture to pat the object of his admiration.

He had to pass the square on his way to school, so every morning he waited on the corner, anxiously and in vain, finding to his dismay that the old man had taken to crossing the road lower down where it was not so wide and where there was a set of traffic lights. Jamie wondered if it was also because he did not want to speak to him again. He came very late in the morning and walked so slowly that if Jamie stood too long at the square waiting for him to reach it he was late for school.

He and Cora usually went to school together, but she could not be bothered to hang about on the street corner waiting for the old man to approach just because he had a horrible, skinny dog that her brother had taken a liking to.

"But you don't understand," said Jamie. "I know he's not very handsome or anything like that but he's a greyhound. A very special one with a pedigree and a long name."

"And you'll get a long page of lines if you're late for school any more. Maybe even the cane. You know what Old Army said last time."

Jamie sighed. "Old Army" was Mr. C. H. Armstrong, headmaster of St. Saviour's Church of England School for Boys and Girls.

St. Saviour's was a very third-rate school. It was grim, square, and tall, a gray building with many windows both broken and dirty, surrounded by rusty iron railings. The interior paintwork was of the standard cream and green, the cream being aged into a far more dismal shade of pale and blotchy brown. The classrooms were still lit by gas and in the winter months it was the job of the monitors to light the lamps with the aid of a long pole. When a teacher was not there to supervise, this pole was more often used as a kind of lance with which to tease friends and annoy enemies and was responsible for many of the broken windows. The walls were smeared with blobs of ink, the outside doors were scrawled over with chalk stolen from the classroom, while the corridors and cloakrooms were more cheerfully decorated in a similar manner with varying shades of lipstick.

Although Jamie was only eleven he was in the top class of the school. This was in no way a compliment to his capabilities but owing to a shortage of teachers, who never stayed longer than it was absolutely necessary—usually just one term—and Jamie's classmates ranged in age between twelve and fifteen. It was a very unruly class and the older boys held a scornful disregard for all forms of discipline and every teacher, which was the main reason for the advent of a new master every term. Most of these were ex-Army men, retired majors and captains, but even they were confounded by their disorderly pupils, although they managed to strike fear into the hearts of on or two even if they taught them nothing.

Jamie was the youngest in the class and he hated being there. No one took much notice of him at first and he tried to learn his lessons in spite of the uproar and the distractions. The girls were mostly as bad as the boys, wearing gaudy clothes, high-heeled shoes, and layers of vivid makeup which they put on in the classroom while the teacher waited patiently for their attention.

Jamie gazed in amazed awe when, for the first time, he watched a girl opposite him contort her lips into what he considered to be peculiar shapes as she carefully applied some almost orange-colored lipstick.

"What you looking at, nosy?" she said rudely, and hastily Jamie looked down at his books, not daring to turn his head in her direction for the rest of the morning.

Cora could not understand why he hated school so much. She was ten, in a class much quieter, with a

teacher stern enough to make even some of the boys in Jamie's class think twice before answering back. She had a special friend, too, and was not shy about joining the other girls' games.

Jamie was shy and often tongue-tied and the lack of anyone in his new class with whom he could possibly be friendly made his diffidence and loneliness even more pronounced. He sat silently through the lessons, some-times concentrating, but lately thinking a great deal about the greyhound.

If he had a dog he would not be lonely. It would not matter if he had no friends. He could talk to a dog and know that it would always be faithful. Dogs were like that. People were not.

In the playground he could talk to Cora. But she was usually busy with a skipping rope or a ball, being very popular with the other girls on account of her good looks and unvarying vivacity. So Jamie invariably stood alone or sat on the steps, hugging his bottle of milk and twisting a straw, dreaming of the day when he would have his own dog, preferably a greyhound like Silver Streak who could win him prizes.

Even then he was not always left in peace. There was a ginger-haired boy in the next form who constantly teased and taunted him. Jamie had once blacked his eye and broken his finger in a fight and the boy had never forgotten it.

His name was Manny Silverman. He was skinny and pimple-faced and always wore leather, fur-lined jackets and long, knife-pleated trousers. He was a year younger than Jamie, with a crowd of followers who backed him in everything he did but left him to take the blame if things went wrong.

He and his gang would circle around Jamie as he sat on the steps and call him names, sometimes throwing their caps at him or trying to grab his if he were wearing one. Jamie did his best to ignore them. It was impossible to fight back. There were too many of them, some from Jamie's own class and old enough to put Manny Silverman in his place but who encouraged him instead.

So Jamie listened to their insults and catcalls in silence, biting his lips to hold back his angry retorts which only gave them encouragement, keeping his clenched fists in his pockets, knowing the futility of trying to fight them all. But he could not always hide the tears of rage which filled his eyes as their taunts became unbearable and, amid shouts of merciless laughter, he would run up the steps and into the classroom, using up his anger by thumping and kicking the desk which was made of wood and could not feel.

One day when he ran up to the classroom he found that he was not alone. Another boy was sitting there with his feet up on a desk, a comic strewn across his knees and a prefect's badge on his lapel. Jamie was too late to withdraw. The boy had seen him.

"Come on in, kid," he said condescendingly. "What's the matter?"

"Nothing," muttered Jamie, and stood twisting the door handle which was loose from having been twisted so often.

"Come off it. What you crying for if there's nothing wrong?"

"I'm not crying. I've got something in my eye."

The prefect laughed.

"Those kids been teasing you again? I know, you needn't tell me. I've heard 'em. You oughn't to take any notice of 'em. That Silverman's no better than you."

"He is when he's got a gang to back him up."

"So what? He don't go home with 'em. You want to get him after school."

Jamie stared at the boy who was offering him helpful advice and listening sympathetically. He had never spoken to any of the boys in his class before but he knew a lot about the one confronting him now.

His name was Hilliard and he was the most popular boy in class. He was not on exactly good terms with the teachers but he had what he called "an understanding" with them. They left him alone and he sometimes helped them keep the class in order. He was the only one who could. When he said: "All right, kids, let the teacher have a say. After all, he's got to earn a living," the class would quieten almost miraculously for half an hour. As far as the teachers were concerned, he did not say it often enough.

Hilliard, who had a foot in both camps, was admired by many and tolerated by those who were afraid to openly dislike him. Uninspiring in appearance, he had very persuasive powers which puzzled Jamie, and a self-confident swagger. Rumor had it that he was an ex-Borstal boy and that St. Saviour's could not expel him because no other school would take him, but there were lots of rumors like that about Hilliard which could be neither confirmed nor denied. Jamie was half afraid of him, wondering at his power, because he did not talk of razors or revenge, nor flash a knife or knuckle-duster, and yet no one ever defied him.

"Well?" said Hilliard.

"It won't help," replied Jamie. "No matter how many times I bash him he'll still be the same. He just don't like me."

"That should worry you. Look, kid, next time he calls you any names just call him a few back and then come and tell me. I'll soon show Mr. Silverman with his fur-lined coats who's boss around here."

"Thanks, Hilliard," said Jamie awkwardly, and forced a grin to his face.

"Think nothing of it. Maybe you can do me a favor one day," and Hilliard smiled.

It was a twisted, triumphant sort of smile, but Jamie recognized it as the smile of friendship only. He suddenly felt that he now had someone to turn to if he ever needed any help. Hilliard was an ally, his friend in a world of strangers, and it was good to have a friend.

2

No Room for a Dog

I

Still Jamie was lonely. After his conversation with Hilliard the older boy sometimes flashed him a grin in the classroom. Nothing else. He never spoke and Jamie did not like to presume upon his kindness. So after a few hopeful days, waiting for a toffee to be slung in his direction, listening for a "Hi, kid," which never came, Jamie went back to dreaming about the dog he was going to have one day and thinking about Silver Streak.

Already he had resigned himself to the fact that he could never own a greyhound. He had little idea of the value of money, but he guessed that Silver would be expensive. Probably a pound or more. To Jamie who rarely had more than sixpence for the Saturday pictures, twenty shillings was a fabulous sum, but he was still determined to have a dog.

If he could get one for about five shillings . . . surely mongrels would not cost more than that. Of course, if he had a friend who had a dog that had puppies he might have been able to get one for nothing. But he didn't have any friends so that idea was not much good.

However, five shillings was not such an impossible sum. If he didn't go to the pictures for ten weeks he would have enough to buy a dog. Oh, the wonder of such a thought! A dog of his very own! No pictures, no "Superman" for ten weeks. It would be well worth it for a dog of his own.

Jamie, sitting in the classroom while the teacher rambled on about vulgar fractions, allowed his imagination to get the better of him.

He was remembering a dog book he had seen in the library the last time he went. It was full of black and white photographs, with all the names in alphabetical order. Some of them had weird names—some of them were weird dogs. He had never seen such animals in the streets of London. Afghan hounds and chihuahuas (he was not even sure how to pronounce them); Bedlingtons and Newfoundlands (he thought that was the name of a country somewhere in America); and more ordinary dogs like poodles and spaniels.

There was another dog similar to the greyhound, called a whippet. It was smaller, and Jamie was very interested. His home was only small, so that a little dog would be the best to have. A whippet was about half the size of a greyhound, he thought, and looked exactly the same but—and he sighed—it would probably cost more than five shillings.

He decided that he would just not have to be particular. Any dog would do, so long as it did not cost more than five shillings. And he would start saving this week. It would not be so hard to start saving now for he had already missed one episode of "Superman" and he still had three halfpence in his pocket. He would start saving this very evening and now, having made up his mind, he was impatient to get home, to find a tin box for his money and to open his account.

He smiled hugely, and the teacher, seeing it, knew that he was not concentrating on vulgar fractions. No one could look that happy about arithmetic, especially Vincent, who was always near the bottom in examinations. But he would have been gratified to know that Jamie was doing arithmetic of a sort, even if he was only working out how many episodes of "Superman" he would have to miss in order to buy his dog.

Next, during history lesson, Jamie tried to think of a name for his dog. It was very difficult because he was greatly biased. Thoughts of Silver Streak kept him constantly occupied. He would have to have a white dog. He would call it Silver. But supposing he couldn't get a white dog? And would it be fair to give it the same name as a dog with a long pedigree? Would it be a compliment or an insult to Silver Streak? Jamie could not decide and eventually he came to the conclusion that it would be best to wait until he had actually bought the dog before giving it a name.

The next thing to trouble him was where to buy it. The dogs in the pet shop looked very extravagant. Poodles, spaniels, collies; they would probably be more than five shillings. Still perhaps they sold mongrels too which they did not show but kept hidden at the back.

Then another thought struck him. It was a very bad one. Supposing his mother said no? Supposing he couldn't persuade her to let him have a dog? She'd just have to say yes. She couldn't say no.

Jamie was so full of his desire to possess a dog that

now he could never forget the idea. He had to have a dog. He needed a dog desperately, and he thought of how the old man walked along the street every morning with Silver Streak. He could never be lonely with a dog like that.

Jamie could picture him in some shabby room, with a gas fire and old coats everywhere, a dingy lamp and a dirty window. The old man would be in his armchair, his scarf still wrapped around him, reading the paper, and at his feet would be the dog. Looking whiter in the firelight, with its thin head stretched on its paws, it would be pressed up close to its master, staring up at him occasionally with those strange yellow eyes, loving him, trusting him.

Thinking like that, Jamie almost cried. His longing to have a dog was so great that his loneliness swept over him in self-pitying waves.

Ten weeks! It was too long, too long.

Five shillings! Such a huge amount and yet so little to buy a lifelong friend.

"When I have my dog," Jamie was saying to himself as he went home. "When I have my dog . . ." and he grinned to himself as he raced along the streets.

He was thinking of a tin box full of sixpences and of a white dog beside the fire.

II

Jamie was sensible to consider having a small dog instead of one as large as Silver Streak, for there was only just enough room at home for him and his family.

Home was a second-floor flat in Paddington. Flat was too grand a name for it, really, because there were only two rooms and a tiny kitchen and it was not even self-contained because the bathroom was on the landing above and shared by everyone else in the house, seven different families in all.

Mr. O'Tooley, with his wife and eighteen-year-old daughter, lived in the basement. He was the landlord and came from County Waterford. Mrs. Kozaki, a Greek Cypriot woman, had a son of Cora's age and rented one room on the ground floor. She was always shouting at the poor boy and Jamie often found him curled up inside the front porch behind the door, with a tear-streaked face, too frightened to go in to his mother. Next door to them was an Indian student, whose name Jamie could never remember and whom he did not see very often.

On the first floor was another Irish family by the name of Doherty. Mr. Doherty was a cousin of Mrs. O'Tooley. He played the trumpet and was not very popular when, on weekdays and up till almost eleven at night, he practiced pieces like the "Post Horn Gallop" or the latest jazz. Nobody minded on Saturdays and Sundays but during the week it was awful. Mrs. Doherty had twin babies and she and Mrs. Vincent spent a lot of time talking about them and Jamie's baby sister Leah, who was only nine months old.

On the floor above Jamie was a family from Sierra Leone by the name of King. Mr. King was a bus conductor and worked with Jamie's father. If they were not on different shifts they went off together to the garage, laughing and joking about nothing in particular, even on the most miserable of days finding something to smile over.

Mrs. King had a job in an office so she never had time to stop and talk with Jamie's mother or Mrs. Doherty, but was forever rushing about; racing for the morning bus, racing home to get dinner before her husband returned from work, racing through the shopping, washing and cleaning on a Saturday so that she could relax on Sunday. No wonder she was thin. She had two sons, Harry and George, but they were both too old to be interested in Jamie, who was far too shy to make any friendly advances in the first place.

The remaining family, on the top floor, were five noisy Italians by the name of Corsini. Mr. Corsini was a thin little man, just the opposite to his wife, who, though small, was shaped like a barrel and had a voice like a parrot. She and Mrs. Kozaki were a fine pair, constantly raving about something or another, and the three children were always squabbling too, making the floors and ceilings shake sometimes as they rolled over and over, locked in angry embrace, pulling out chunks of curly black hair and calling each other names in Italian.

Jamie was the quietest child in the house and, although Cora knew all the Italians, said hello to George and Harry, smiled at Andreas Kozaki and always remembered the Indian's name, he could never overcome his shyness with any of them.

When Jamie got home that evening he hardly noticed Andreas sobbing quietly in the hall. He raced up the shadowy staircase, scarcely pausing to recover when he caught his foot in the broken linoleum, and burst into the livingroom, grinning widely.

"Well, well!" exclaimed Mrs. Vincent from the little kitchen. "What's got into you today? Why are you racing about like that? Have you fallen down those stairs again?"

Jamie stopped grinning, suddenly realizing the great importance of what he had to ask and wanting to create a favorable impression. He straightened his tie, pulled up his socks and strolled nonchalantly into the kitchen, which was no more than a corner screened off from the rest of the livingroom.

"What's for tea?" he wanted to know, and peered into a saucepan, lifting up the lid and drawing back his head sharply as a cloud of stream rose up in his face.

"Now put that back!" cried Mrs. Vincent. "Just you wait and see. But what are you up to, Jamie? Have you done something wrong?"

She frowned, eyeing her son suspiciously, sensing that something had happened but unable to decide what it was. He was after something, that was sure, but whether it was a pardon or a present she did not know.

"Come on," she urged. "Tell me. What have you been doing?"

"Nothing, Mum. Honest," and now that it had come to the point Jamie found it very difficult to say what he wanted to say.

He had to put it the right way, not just suddenly say, "I want a dog," because then she would exclaim no without thinking. And if he said, "Can I have a dog?" she would say no, too. This thing would have to be done very carefully, persuasively. He would have to make her see what an asset a little dog could be.

"Mum . . . d'you know anything about greyhounds?"

"Greyhounds! Lord, what questions you ask! How should I know anything about greyhounds?"

"Dad once bet some money on a greyhound," he reminded her.

"And lost it, too. They're dangerous animals, Jamie, and lead a man to ruin. You're not thinking of putting money on dogs, I hope."

"No, Mum. I've got no money. But I see a man every day who has a greyhound called Silver Streak and this greyhound has a pedigree and a wonderful long name and he wins prizes and things and runs races and——"

"Jamie," broke in his mother. "What's all this leading up to? You're not just telling me about greyhounds for nothing."

"Well . . ."

He hesitated, not daring to look into his mother's demanding eyes for fear that he should see denial in them before he had finished uttering the words. He pulled the lid off another pot and drew back with wrinkled nose as the smell of boiling cabbage assailed him.

"Ugh! Cabbage! You won't give me none, will you, Mum?"

"You'll eat what I give you. Cabbage is good for you and you'll eat it."

Jamie plucked up all his courage, suddenly seeing an opening.

"Mum . . . If I eat all my cabbage every day and if I

go shopping for you and help Cora with the washing-up and clean the shoes and don't get my clothes dirty, can I have something?"

"Now we're coming around to the truth," said Mrs. Vincent with a smile. "Well, what do you want this time?"

"Promise me first," demanded Jamie. "I promise to do all those things I just said if you promise too."

"I'll make no promises till you tell me what you want."

Jamie held his breath. It was impossible to compromise with his mother. She would either say yes to the dog and not insist that he ate his cabbage, did the shopping, and cleaned the shoes, or she would say no and expect him to do those things anyway.

"Mum, can I have a dog, please?"

He did not wait for her answer, seeing it already.

"Just a little one, really small, no trouble and nothing to feed. Please . . . just a tiny one," and his voice faded into nothing because she was shaking her head.

"Jamie," she sighed. "Answer me one thing. Just where would we put a dog?"

"He wouldn't take up much room. Not a little one. He could sleep on my bed."

"Little dogs grow, Jamie, like little babies. And they take care and feeding, not just bits and pieces. Even if we had the room we can't afford a dog, Jamie. They eat as much as you do."

"I'd eat less!" cried Jamie, a heavy pain gnawing into his heart so that already he did not feel hungry. "Please

don't say no, Mum. Please let me have one. Please, please, please."

"It's no good crying, Jamie," said his mother, noticing the tears moistening in his eyes. "We can't afford a dog and that's all there is to it."

Jamie said no more. He turned slowly from the kitchen and wandered back into the livingroom. It looked a mess, as usual, with the baby's toys scattered on the floor and on the sofa; the table laid for tea, cluttered up with sauce and pickle bottles, half a pint of milk, a tin of cream, and Leah's orange juice; the washing hanging from a short line over in one corner by the window and the curtains blowing in the breeze because both windows were open.

Jamie did not notice the untidiness. He saw everything through a blur of tears and he was breathing hard to hold them back because he did not want to cry. But there was such a pain in his heart, pain of emptiness and disappointment; hope being crushed; loneliness overwhelming him. He wanted a dog so badly—a tiny, tiny one would do.

He walked over to a window, clutched at the billowing curtain, and hung on to it. He stared out on to the darkening street and the lights shining from the lampposts looked long and streaky through his tears. He blinked and they became normal but only for a second. He heard his mother saying something but ignored her.

She was just being mean, not letting him have a dog. She did not care that he was lonely and without friends.

He thought of how he had been planning his dog all afternoon. He remembered how happy he had been, how he had run all the way home, how he had intended to find an old cocoa or coffee tin in which to save his money, and the tears rolled faster and faster down his cheeks until he could feel them trickling under his collar and around his neck.

He could not have a dog. He told himself that over and over again. He must stop thinking about it. There was no room for a dog.

A short moan escaped his lips as he thought that. No room for a dog. There was room for him, Cora, and Leah in this tiny place.

His mother thought he was sulking by the window and called: "Now, Jamie, it's no good acting spoiled. You can't have a dog and that's that. And stop pulling at the curtain or you'll have it down on your head."

Jamie let go of the curtain. He thought of the greyhound and the old man, somewhere in the warm. Was it so bad to want something as he wanted a dog?

He sniffed several times and wiped his eyes on his sleeve. The pain was fading a little now, dull despair overcoming the shock of disappointment and disbelief. His mother had said that there was no room and he knew that it was no good asking again.

3

Silver

I

Jamie did not surrender his dream of having a dog but
he kept it to himself. He stopped going to school with
Cora in the mornings because she complained so much
when he waited by the square for the old man and Silver Streak to come by, sometimes drenched with rain
and often shivering with cold.

The disappointment when the old man did not come was almost as bad as when his mother had said he could not have a dog. He would stare along the street in disbelief, expecting him to appear every minute, the shine fading from his eyes, the hope fading from his heart when nothing happened. Luckily this was not often. The old man kept regular habits and it was only when it was very wet that he did not come.

He grew accustomed to seeing Jamie waiting for him and, although for a couple of weeks he did nothing but stare belligerently at him, one morning he actually acknowledged his presence.

"Shouldn't you be at school?" he said gruffly, but before Jamie could reply was already walking on.

It took longer to get the greyhound even slightly interested in him. Every morning Jamie clicked his tongue, snapped his fingers, whistled or uttered a soft, "Hello boy," but the dog completely ignored him, often turning the other way or burying his head closer into the old man's dusty coat. Once when Jamie leaned down to pat him he cringed and side-jumped as if expecting some hurt, and for two days following that he stepped into the road rather than pass Jamie on the pavement.

Jamie could not understand him. He felt sure that the old man did not ill-treat him. What would be the point of having a dog for a companion and treating him badly? Admittedly, his master showed him no affection, but Jamie knew that some dogs preferred it that way, especially if they were accustomed to undemonstrative owners. Perhaps he just did not like strangers—but surely he couldn't consider Jamie to be a stranger by now?

Three weeks went by like this and during that time Jamie saved his money, hope burning eternally within him, if in secret. He rescued a baked-bean tin from the dustbin, washed it, and kept his sixpences in it, counting them occasionally as if by doing so he could increase their value, but after three weeks it was still only one and sevenpence halfpenny and did not seem very much.

Jamie stayed patient all that time, trying not to think of his dog—the one he was going to have—but concentrating all his thoughts on the greyhound—the unobtainable. He could love it without possessiveness and, therefore, without pain . . . or so he believed.

April was nearly over when Jamie eventually became on speaking terms with the old man. The trees in the square did not look so drab. The leaves were bright green and numerous and there were clouds of pink and white blossoms dangling over the railings, with fragrant petals crushed into the pavement and trailing along the gutter. The earth smelt damp and fresh. A gardener had spent a week turning over the soil and Jamie was surprised to see that it was black and clean instead of the usual dusty gray.

Disturbed worms had crawled from the flower beds on to the pavement and some lay dry and hopeless while others were squashed and dead. Jamie felt sorry for them and when he saw them lying there he would gently pick them up, stroke the dirt from their skiny brown skins and drop them through the railings on to the earth, hoping no bird would find them before they burrowed underground.

Once he took one home, intending to keep it as a pct.

A boy at school had told him how you could train grass snakes to do tricks and Jamie had hopes of teaching his little worm to glide through his fingers and take food from them. He kept him in a flower pot on the window sill, but one morning his mother accidentally knocked the pot down. It smashed into the area, and, although Jamie ran down immediately to search for half an hour for his worm, he could not find it. However, it was no great loss and before the day was over he had forgotten all about it.

He could not forget about Silver Streak, though, and one Saturday morning decided that he must speak to the old man again, ask him some questions about his dog and perhaps, if everything went well, he might ask for permission to take him for a walk sometimes. That would be wonderful, but he wouldn't take him to the square. He would take him to Hyde Park and the Serpentine.

He remembered how he watched people with their dogs on Sunday mornings in the park. The old ladies with their pekes and poodles, the boys with their mongrels. He preferred watching the latter, for they always had much more fun, throwing sticks and balls into the lake for the dogs to retrieve, racing about and wrestling in the grass with them, having a tug-of-war, the boy shouting, the dog growling.

How he would love to do all these things with a dog of his own, but even then he doubted if Silver Streak would want to do them with him. He didn't seem to be that kind of a dog, but maybe that was because he lived with an old man. If he went out with Jamie he would be different. He would be young again. Jamie wondered how old he was.

When the old man came along that last Saturday morning in April, Jamie was very bold. He stepped in front of him so that he would have to stop and said, "Please, sir, how old is Silver Streak?"

The old man looked surprised. His watery gray eyes widened and he looked down on Jamie as if wondering what it was confronting him.

"How do you know my dog's name?" he said.

"You told me, long time ago, what it was."

"I don't remember. I told you, did I?" and he shook his head, either denying the fact or trying to clear his memory. "And you remembered?"

"Of course, sir. He's a real beautiful dog. How could I forget?"

The old man started walking again and Jamie walked along beside him, smiling up at him and refusing to be discouraged by the peevishness of his expression.

"How old is he?" he asked again.

"You like dogs, don't you, laddie?" said the old man, ignoring the question or not hearing it. "Aren't you the little fellow who stands here every day when he should be at school?"

Jamie was thrilled. He remembered. He did see him and take notice.

"That's right. Every day."

"What for?"

"To see Silver Streak of course. I couldn't bear not to see him every day."

"Why? What's so special about my dog that you have to see him every day?"

"Well, I don't know," said Jamie thoughtfully. It was difficult to explain how he felt about Silver Streak. How he had pretended sometimes that the greyhound was his and how seeing him made the feeling more realistic. The old man might laugh and he would never understand.

"I just like seeing him," he finished lamely. "I've never seen a greyhound before."

They had reached the gate by now and the old man was delving into his pocket for the key. He could not find it and mumbled angrily to himself as he felt along every lining and then again through his coat pockets.

"Here, hold this," he said and, to Jamie's surprise and pleasure, pushed the string attached to the greyhound's collar into his hand. Jamie held on tight, gazing down on the dog as if it really belonged to him now. He hoped the old man would be a long time finding the key and while he searched, slowly undoing his buttons and feeling through his inside pockets, Jamie stretched down a hand to stroke the greyhound.

Silver Streak saw the hand descending to his back and he cringed down low, gazing up at the boy with those odd yellow eyes of his. He did not step away this time, as if acknowledging the boy's right to touch him while he held the string, but his eyes seemed to beg Jamie not to stroke him. Jamie refused to notice their pleading. He just had to touch the dog.

Gently he placed his hand on the greyhound's bony

back. Softly he smoothed along the bumpy spine. Carefully he felt the hollow flanks with his fingers.

The dog trembled violently. His whole frame shook as if convulsed with fever and he cringed so low that his belly was almost touching the pavement.

Jamie was frightened. He pulled his hand away and put it in his pocket. "What's the matter, boy?" he crooned in his softest voice. "I haven't hurt you. Good boy. Good boy. Don't be scared."

Gradually the dog ceased to shake. He stood up again and sidled over to the old man, pressing himself against his legs, but his eyes stared up into the boy's, and Jamie felt ashamed. There was such reproach in the dog's eyes that Jamie found himself unable to return the gaze.

He suddenly became aware of the fact that he was completely ignorant about dogs. Until this moment he had looked upon them as animals, more intelligent, friendly, and comforting than all the rest, but inferior nevertheless. But there was something about Silver's eyes, the depth of despair or loneliness within them, that made him realize that this dog had known life more than he had; that he was a stumbling fool who could see no farther than his own desire and that now the dog, tolerant of his existence before, had withdrawn from him completely.

He was angry with himself for touching the dog. Just when there had been hope of gaining his confidence he had blundered badly. He had ignored the warning and received his just reward. The dog did not look at him again. He kept to the far side of his master and turned his back to Jamie.

The old man had found the key by this time and after unlocking the rusty gate he took the string from Jamie's hand and went into the square. He stared uncertainly at Jamie for a moment or two and then said, "Well, are you coming in or aren't you?" and Jamie needed no second bidding.

II

Lying in bed that night, Jamie could not sleep. His mind went over and over the events of the morning and he smiled involuntarily as he thought of them. Altogether it had been very strange and slightly unbelievable.

The old man was interested in Jamie and wanted to talk to him. He untied the string from the dog's collar and left him to wander about at will. He himself turned in the direction of the summer house and, uncertainly, Jamie followed him.

"So," said the old man when they were seated, "you're interested in my dog, are you?"

"Yes," said Jamie. "Very."

"And you want to know how old he is?"

"And lots of other things too."

The old man chuckled. Jamie was surprised. He had such a miserable face that Jamie thought him incapable of being amused.

"Ah, you're just like me when I was a lad. Couldn't keep my eyes off dogs," he said. "Every blessed dog I ever saw I had to touch and call to. And I've paid for it in my time. The bites I've had! Nearly lost my thumb once. A great Airedale it was, vicious brute. Everybody told me not to touch it."

He chuckled again and there was a faraway look in his eyes as he thought back over the years, recalling dogs, horses, and old friends.

Jamie listened and watched the greyhound.

Silver Streak was doing nothing in particular. He sniffed at a rhododendron bush, examined the newly turned earth with vague interest, watched a sparrow hop from railing to railing with slight surprise, and stared in the direction of his master several times, as if wishing to be in the summer house with him instead of being forced to wander about in the square with nothing to do.

Jamie felt his boredom. Poor thing. There could be nothing in this square to interest him after all this time and he began to wonder if there had ever been anything to stir his soul. He wasn't like an ordinary dog that dug holes, rolled in the grass, and chased after cats. He seemed so utterly bored with life, shut up within himself, frustrated.

Jamie guessed that he did not race any more. He wondered if Silver missed his old life, the kennels and the excitement, the fullness of those days. It must be strange for a sporting dog to tread the city pavements as he did, with only an old man for company who rarely spoke.

He suddenly became aware of the old man's voice again. He was talking about the First World War now and the horses; how they were blown to bits by shells;

how they still trusted their masters when they had gaping wounds in their necks and flanks; how they trudged through the mud and the rain like the soldiers, faced the same dangers, and died on the same battlefields.

Jamie listened, both horrified and thrilled. His respect for animals grew while he listened and he learned that they were noble.

Then his thoughts went back to the lonely dog again and he knew that Silver Streak must feel like him; empty and sometimes afraid. Perhaps he wanted a friend too.

Listening to the old man, he began to understand the dog, for he could sense that the old man was lonely too, missing his friends of bygone days, missing the horses of the war years, still living in the past. Jamie felt sorry for him. He felt sorry for them both and he learned a lot that morning, just listening to the old man and watching the dog.

Time passed very quickly but neither noticed it. The sun was bright, throwing long shadows across the new grass in the square, shining down on the rhododendron leaves and exposing the dust which gathered along every vein. Sparrows busied themselves in the middle of the lawn, squabbling pugnaciously, feeling the warmth of the sun and making the most of it. A ginger cat slunk stealthily through the railings, eyeing the greyhound distrustfully, but Silver did not notice it.

He stared longingly at his master in the summer house, wishing that he was not banished into the sunshine, but with dutiful halfheartedness he nibbled a few long blades of grass which the lawn mower had missed, then sat and licked his paws.

"Well," said the old man at last, stirring slowly from his corner, "I suppose I must be moving. I've enjoyed talking to you, young man. We must meet again some time."

"I was wondering," began Jamie carefully, "I was wondering if perhaps sometimes I could take Silver Streak for a walk. I'd be very careful with him. You could trust me for sure."

He looked down at his shoes, biting his lip. He expected the old man to say no. It was wisest to anticipate nothing.

"Where would you take him?" the old man wanted to know.

Jamie stared up hopefully. "To the park. There's lots of room there and he could come to no harm."

"All right, then," said the old man. "To the park it is." He sighed. "I can never manage to get there myself these days. I try but somehow . . . I'm getting old, old. . . ."

The distant look was returning to his eyes again, but he checked it as he recognized the eager hopefulness in the young boy's face.

"When are you going there? Tomorrow perhaps, tomorrow morning?"

Tomorrow morning! This was too wonderful to be true. The old man was saying yes. . . .

And now, lying in the semi-darkness of the bedroom, with the street lamps glowing gloomily through the thin curtains, it seemed to Jamie that the morning would never come.

4

Never "My Dog"

I

The old man lived in a shabby house in a street not far from the square. Faded green paint peeled from the door and window frames and there was a large black knocker, shaped like a lion's head, instead of the usual bells. The old man had told Jamie to knock twice very loudly and he did so, not without difficulty because the knocker was only just within his reach when he stood on tiptoe.

It seemed a long time before he heard footsteps shuffling down the stairs and could make out through the patterned glass panels on either side of the door the dark shadow of a figure looming in the hallway. The door opened and Jamie grinned widely. The old man just stared at him, his pale gray eyes completely blank, as if he had forgotten who he was for a moment.

"Hello," said Jamie, but his smile faded because for some unknown reason he was a little afraid of the old man when he stared like that. "I've come for the dog."

Still the old man stared, saying nothing.

"Silver Streak," said Jamie. "You said I could take him out this morning."

"The dog? Oh . . . yes. Come in, come in," and his voice was flat, blank like his eyes, and Jamie almost felt a cold draft within him, as if his friendship had been rebuffed, as if the old man did not want him to take the dog out after all. Suddenly he wished he had not come, wished that he had never met Silver Streak, wished that yesterday had never happened. He had looked forward so much to this morning that the anticipation had been greater than the actual fact.

Silently, miserably, he followed the old man up the stairs. He lived right at the top of the house in a little back room which smelled of stale fruit and dog. Silver was lying across the old man's unmade bed, his long thin muzzle resting on his paws, his yellow eyes half closed in gloomy meditation. He opened them wider as Jamie entered the room, stared distantly at him for a moment or two, then let them droop again. Jamie felt even more lost and alone.

"Well," said the old man. "There he is. If he'll go with you, that is."

"You don't mind me taking him out, do you? If you'd rather I didn't . . ."

"Do what you like. Look . . ." He paused, looked around the room, and pointed to his coat which was flopped over a shabby, tall-backed chair. "In the pocket there you'll find some string," he said. "Tie that to his collar and he'll go with you. Come back when you like. No hurry."

Jamie found the string and tied it to Silver's collar. Silver did nothing. He did not even raise his head while Jamie fumbled with the knot. Jamie felt very shy and stupid. He wanted to say something to the dog but could think of nothing. It seemed ridiculous not to know what to say to a dog. Even more he wished he had not come this morning. Seeing Silver every day, planning how it would be in his company, thinking of the pleasure of a dog of his own—all this had been far more wonderful than tying a bit of string to a reluctant greyhound in a shabby, smelly room with a truculent old man gazing absently at him. He felt like a trespasser there and he stood staring down at Silver, wishing the dog would show some sign of pleasure or at least acknowledge his existence.

At last he said: "Come on, Silver boy. We're going for a walk."

He felt sure that this word would do the trick. He had seen how other dogs reacted at the mention of "walk." They jumped about, barked, went wild with joy, as if a walk was the most wonderful thing in the life of a dog. Silver did none of these things. He opened his eyes again, yawned widely, stared at Jamie, and rose slowly from the bed. Jamie inwardly breathed a sigh of relief. At least he knew the meaning of the word.

He gave an awkward "goodbye" to the old man and walked carefully down the stairs, the string clutched tightly in his left hand, feeling depressed instead of happy, almost wishing that the walk were over instead of only just begun.

But when he reached the front door and could breathe fresh air again, see the sun shining down from a blue but cloudy sky, and a couple of fat gray pigeons strutting about in the gutter, his spirits soared because it was a lovely day and he was taking a dog for a walk for the first time.

He shut the door quietly behind him. There was no one in the street. It was half-past ten and nearly everyone was either still in bed or only just getting up. The sun gleamed and sparkled on window panes, daffodils spread gay splashes of yellow in different parts of the street, and a black cat sat on the pavement, sunning himself and watching the pigeons. Apart from the cat, Jamie was alone with the dog, completely alone, and now once again he was happy.

He sat down on the doorstep, drawing the string up short so that Silver could not sidle away, and he stared lovingly at the dirty white greyhound, thinking of all the things he wanted to say to him, grinning with pleasure.

Silver slowly sat down. He returned Jamie's stare, but watched his hands too, as if afraid that they would reach out to touch him again. But Jamie was taking no chances. He was going to be very careful this time and make no mistakes. From now on he and Silver were going to be friends.

"Silver," he said, "you're a real nice dog."

Silver stared beyond him at the shabby door, neither pricking his ears nor changing the expression in his eyes.

"Hey, Silver," Jamie tried again. "Silver. What's the matter with you? Don't you like walks? Silver."

The greyhound looked at the milk bottles beside Jamie on the doorstep. He seemed determined to ignore the boy and showed no recognition of his name. But Jamie was not upset. He was a little puzzled but he was patient too. The whole morning stretched ahead and he was

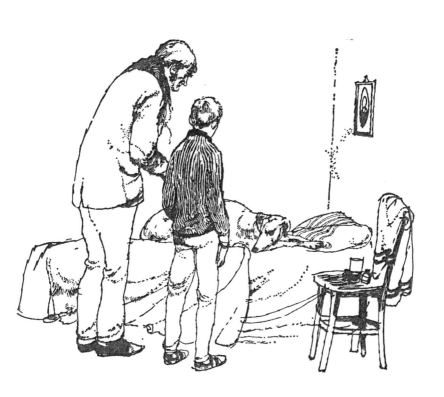

determined to give the greyhound the best time he had ever had in his life.

He jumped up from the step, dusted the seat of his trousers automatically, and set off. Silver did not follow and Jamie felt the jerk of the string in his hand. He looked around, surprised to see that Silver was still sitting in the same position, not looking at the milk bottles but staring at Jamie.

"Come on, boy," he said. "What's the matter?"

He pulled gently at the string, coaxing him again and again, but Silver would not move. He whistled, snapped his fingers, tugged harder on the string, called and called, but Silver stayed exactly where he was. Jamie began to feel silly and he was glad that there was no one in the street to see his plight. This was stupid.

"Come on, Silver," he begged. "A walk, don't you want a walk? I won't hurt you. I won't steal you. I'll bring you back home afterwards. Good boy, come on."

Silver just stared but did not move. At least five minutes passed in this way and Jamie's embarrassment was changing to anger. The dog was completely stupid, feelingless, or deaf, and he became just as determined to make Silver go for a walk as the greyhound was to stay on the doorstep.

He clenched his teeth and took hold of the string with both hands.

"Look here, dog," he said. "You're coming to the park with me if I have to drag you all the way. Now come on," and he jerked hard on the string with all his strength so that Silver could not resist.

The greyhound rose slowly, ignoring the angry jerks

at his collar, but taking a few hesitant steps in Jamie's direction.

"There's a good boy," said Jamie encouragingly. "Just keep it up, just keep it up."

He pulled again because the greyhound stopped and looked back at the door, and Silver Streak took a few more unsure steps behind him.

In this manner Jamie and the dog eventually reached the end of the street, Silver reluctant, the boy determined.

Then, when the corner was turned and the old man's house was out of sight, Silver seemed decided to make the best of a bad job. He stopped pulling against Jamie and followed obediently, the string hanging slack between them.

Jamie breathed a sigh of relief. Perhaps Silver was shy. He was shy so he should be able to understand the dog. But Jamie could not understand Silver. He spoke to him several times, joyfully, questioningly, sometimes just speaking his name over and over again, but Silver did not look at him. He walked along, picking his way carefully around puddles and damp patches, ignoring Jamie and everything else. He might have been blind or deaf, without smell or sense of feeling. Was there nothing to stir him? Was there no way by which Jamie could gain his friendship or trust? That was how it seemed as they walked along the deserted streets that Sunday morning.

When they reached the park they walked on the grass. Silver sniffed for a moment or two and chewed a few blades of grass with wrinkled nose and distasteful expression. Other dogs raced by. Some stopped to greet the greyhound but Silver took no interest in them and at times seemed half afraid of their intentions. He stepped hesitantly backwards when they came near him and Jamie, pitying him, shooed the strangers away.

But although Silver was such a miserable companion, already Jamie's loneliness was beginning to fade. He could talk out loud without people looking strangely at him, and the very act of being with another living creature entirely alone, especially one that he loved, filled him with a contentment he had never known before. His face shone with happiness and, after a while, he broke into a run, urging Silver to follow him.

"Come on, boy, come on," but he slowed to a puzzled halt when Silver did not keep up with him.

"What's the matter, Silver boy? Don't you like running?" and he dropped on to one knee beside the dog, staring at him, puzzled and disappointed.

Silver stood still, head turned away from Jamie, but for once he seemed unafraid of the closeness of the boy. Jamie gently put one hand across the dog's back, and although Silver quivered a little he did not cringe away. A surge of pity filled Jamie as he kneeled in the grass beside the dog, talking to him, pleading with him, trying to understand him.

He moved his hand slowly to the dog's head, fondling his ears which were soft and loose, noticing the narrowness of the dirty white skull, feeling the hardness of the bones. There was pleasure in stroking the dog thus, especially when Silver did not recoil from his touch, and in those few minutes Jamie noticed more about the greyhound than he had on all previous occasions.

There was a chip of skin missing from his muzzle,

only very tiny. His black nose was dry and patterned with dust. Jamie touched the scar and the nose, and he rubbed his hands more firmly around the thin head, growing in confidence, growing in love. At last Silver turned to look at him, his yellow eyes staring squarely into Jamie's gray ones, and for the first time Jamie knew that he had broken through the dog's self-imposed veneer.

Silver was not afraid of him any more, did not dislike him, did not object to his touch, and Jamie wanted to hold the dog in his arms, crush him to his breast, kiss him. But he didn't do any of those things because he knew that Silver would not approve.

"Silver, Silver, you beautiful dog. If only, if only you were mine," and Silver returned his gaze, accepting his friendship as if having reached the conclusion that it could do him no harm.

II

For several Sundays after that Jamie took Silver to the park. They went out early at eight or nine o'clock, before there were many people about.

The park was beautiful now, the grass soft and green, the trees blossoming with the first summer leaves. Baby ducks splashed in and out of the shadows thrown across the lake by weeping willows; young gray cygnets watched their antics with ill-disguised envy, but too much afraid of their disdainful parents to attempt to join their games; beady-eyed water hens hurried busily to and fro among them. Early swimmers, early boaters, and lone dogs also frequented the lake and Jamie and Silver watched them all with pure contentment.

Silver was too old to race about like the younger dogs. At first Jamie had been disappointed but now he did not mind. There was as much pleasure to be gained by just sitting beside him in the grass, his hand resting across the white skull, feeling the warmth it exuded, and looking happily at each other, sharing the pleasure of being no longer alone.

It seemed a silly way of passing the time and dull to tell of. Sitting in the grass, doing nothing. What pleasure could be obtained like that? But Jamie found pleasure and so did Silver. Sometimes the old dog licked the boy's fingers; gently, slowly, gingerly at first, as if it were something he had not done for a long time and wasn't sure whether it was allowed.

Then, as they grew to know each other better and Silver learned to trust the boy, his affection for Jamie became stronger and it was not enough just to lick his fingers. He licked his face, his shoes, his trousers, snuffled his nose in Jamie's jacket and around his neck, while the boy laughed with delight and sometimes because Silver tickled him. The old dog wagged his tail, rolled over in the grass, wriggling. He looked five years younger already and his black nose was no longer dry and dusty, nor his eyes so dull. They were softer now and they watched Jamie constantly, the smallest move he made registering in the dog's eyes. If Jamie laughed Silver's eyes gleamed. If he were moody Silver's eyes were sad or anxious. On these occasions he would paw at Jamie, whining softly in his throat, nudging him and trying to stir him from his mood.

But Jamie was not often moody, only when he remembered that Silver belonged to the old man and not to him. If only Silver were his dog. The old man did not love him—not as Jamie loved him, anyway. Did Silver love the old man?

These mornings alone with Silver were not enough. Jamie tried to pretend that Silver was his dog but it was hard to forget that he wasn't. Not until they turned homeward did Jamie become depressed. He took Silver back to the old man, then walked miserably along the streets to his own front door, still feeling the shadow of the dog behind him, still wanting to talk to him or stroke him, lost and unhappy without him there.

Above all his happiness with Silver, Jamie's discontentment grew. He wanted a dog of his very, very own, not that of another man. He wanted to feed him, groom him, have him all day long, find him waiting at home when he returned from school, be able to talk about him to others and say, "My dog Silver . . . my dog."

Because he was honest all he could ever say now was, "This dog I take out," never "My dog," and as the days and weeks passed Jamie's sullen moods became more frequent. He wanted something he could not have, he wanted it desperately, and having Silver alone for just a few hours on a Sunday was becoming more of a torment to him than a pleasure. When he saw other boys with their own dogs he felt almost sick with envy.

Every weekend he put his sixpence picture money in the old baked-bean tin. He kept the tin a secret because he did not want his mother to know that he was saving for a dog and on Saturday morning, instead of going to the pictures, he took Silver for a walk or, if that was impossible, he wandered about the streets or up and down the counters in Woolworth's until it was time to go home.

III

Jamie's desire for a dog of his own became so urgent that the money in his box did not add up quickly enough and he began missing out his school dinner once or twice a week, adding the daily ninepence to his collection. It was difficult to keep this secret from Cora because she looked out for him in the dining hall, but once, when she asked him where he had been, he said that he did not like school dinners and that he bought himself some chips and a bar of chocolate. He had to tell the teacher that he went home to lunch and, although sometimes he felt terribly hungry, the pain of hunger was bearable because very soon he would have his dog.

He was determined to have a dog but he said nothing more to his mother, except on odd occasions when he would wistfully remark, "Wouldn't it be lovely to have a dog," just to test her reaction and see if she would weaken. She never did and he didn't mention it to his father. If his mother said no, then his father would say no. However, he had optimistically formed the opinion that if he brought home a sweet and tiny puppy his mother would love it so much that she would not be able to refuse. And, anyway, she could hardly turn it out of the house.

Sometimes Jamie felt a little guilty taking out Silver

and thinking of another dog. But he stopped thinking too much about the future, about what would happen to Silver if he stopped taking him out; that he would miss Silver very much; that Silver might miss him. Instead he daily counted his pennies, sixpences, and shillings until one day they added up to the grand total of eight shillings.

This to Jamie was a fortune. He could buy a really grand dog for that amount and he knew just the place to go for it, too. The old man had talked to him often of Club Row in the City, a Sunday-morning market where they sold just about everything from fleas to elephants and also dogs, and Jamie, on making inquiries, found that he could take a Number Eight bus either from Edgware Road or Oxford Street right there.

When Jamie had eight shillings he thought that was plenty, but he put off going to Club Row for several weeks. Every Sunday morning he took out Silver and he felt like a traitor. But he could never buy Silver and he had to have a dog of his own, so, although he said nothing to the old man, he decided that at the end of May he would give up Silver, not take him out again.

On that last day Silver knew there was something wrong. Jamie was very silent and when Silver nuzzled against him he replied to the gesture halfheartedly, patting him lightly on the shoulder and saying, "Good boy."

They walked slowly through the park, both withdrawn. Jamie thought of the following Sunday, of the puppy that would be his; Silver was morose, not understanding the boy's mood. Jamie was also ashamed of himself.

He took Silver home early that last day and the dog

wagged his tail just a little, nervously, as if he knew that he was banished from Jamie's company and was bewildered by it. He looked at Jamie with pleading in his yellow eyes then jumped up on his master's bed, leaning his muzzle on his paws, watching Jamie as he said goodbye to the old man.

Jamie could almost feel the dog's eyes on him and the thoughts of the puppy he was going to buy next Sunday did not give him the same pleasure any more. But he made himself believe that everything would be all right, once he had the dog, and that he would soon forget Silver.

5

Dogs for Sale

I

Club Row was to Jamie both fascinating and frightening. He stepped off the bus into a puddle, half a dozen others pushing behind him impatiently, while on the pavement people hurried by in twos and threes, some carrying cages, some with rose bushes under their arms, the roots wrapped in soggy newspaper, some with puppies tucked inside their coats.

Jamie was too bewildered at first to take notice of anything, not even the puppies, but seeing the crowds he automatically pushed his left hand into his trouser pocket, clutching at his precious seven and sixpence halfpenny, which was all he had left after paying his fare. Already people were bumping against him and he had not even reached the first big crowds or stalls, and feeling lost and tiny he pressed back against the wall, watching with eyes wide and mouth half open.

He looked right and left, gradually beginning to notice the things about him, and when he had overcome his bewilderment he too became part of the hurrying mass, making toward the first of the stalls to look for his puppy. Jamie's intention of just buying the puppy and going straight home with it soon faded. There was so much to see, so much to hear, so many things to examine and wonder at. This was not just an animal market; they sold anything and everything; and, although he was determined to spend no money until he had bought the dog of his choice, Jamie decided to look about first.

There were five or six stalls offering puppies for sale and Jamie wandered from one to another, heart overwhelmed with love and desire as he fondled the squirming creatures. The first man he came to had three Alsatians, two spaniels, and a fox terrier. The terrier was half buried under a bundle of wood wool, shivering with cold. The spaniels romped about, snarling and biting playfully at each other, while the three Alsatians watched with slight curiosity and disdain. Jamie didn't like the Alsatians much. They were rather wishy-washy in coloring, not quite brown, and they looked very stupid. He stroked the terrier, but at his touch the frightened creature burrowed still farther into the wood wool, whimpering softly.

"Want him, sonny? Lovely pup," said the man, and he grabbed the dog by the scruff of its neck, holding it up for Jamie to examine. He rubbed its hair up the wrong way. "Look, no fleas," he said. "Genuine pup that, sonny. Only a quid. Nine weeks old and house trained."

Jamie silently shook his head, wishing that the man had left the pup in the straw. A whole pound! But then it was a pure-bred dog. The mongrels would be cheaper.

The man dropped the pup back into the wood wool, parted the snarling spaniels, and turned his back to Jamie, saying, "If you ain't buying, don't touch."

Jamie hurriedly went to the next stall. Ten or twelve people were crushed around it and he could not see what was being offered for sale. He pushed and wriggled his way through a narrow gap between two men, only to find that the stall contained nothing but kittens. There were more Alsatians on the third stall, smaller than the first lot with pedigrees supplied. They were five pounds each and Jamie's hopes began to fade.

He went on to the next stall. At last! Eight or ten pups of no particular breed and various colors. A girl of his own age held one in her arms. She was kissing it, stroking it, and cooing over it.

"Oh, Daddy, isn't he sweet," she said, looking up with shining eyes at the man beside her. "Please buy him for me, Daddy. Please."

"But, Sally, where can we keep him? Put him down now and come along. You know what Mummy said. You can't have a dog."

"But I want one," she said, and her whole expression changed. Her smile became a pout and she stamped the ground with her foot, crushing the puppy so tightly that he yelped as he squirmed in her arms. Jamie stared with surprise. She had such a sweet face.

"Remember what happened to the last one," said her father, still adamant. "They're more trouble than they're worth."

"I want it, I want it!" screamed Sally, and tears of anger loomed in her eyes.

Her father sighed.

"How much?" he asked the owner.

"That one? Shetland sheepdog, that. Twenty bob and you've got yourself a bargain."

Jamie knew little about dogs, but he knew that dog

was not a Shetland sheepdog. However, he enviously watched Sally walk away with it, wrapping it tenderly inside her overcoat, and heard her father say, "Well, if this one gets run over it's the last time I'll buy you a dog." Jamie wondered just how long the pretty little thing would live.

He sighed. The stallholder heard him because so far Sally had been his only customer, and now that she had gone Jamie was alone at his stall.

"Lovely dogs," he said. "Man's best friend. You got a dog?"

"No," said Jamie.

"How about one of these?"

He took a couple in his hand at random. The pups were small and his hands were large. The two of them, mostly terrier, looked tinier still crushed together back to back.

"Here, hold 'em," he said, and pushed them into Jamie's arms.

Jamie needed no second bidding. He caressed them gently, pressing his head against the warm, soft bodies. They smelled clean and Jamie in that moment loved them both. All too soon the man took them from him and dropped them back in the straw.

"Want one?" he asked. "Lovely dogs."

"They're beautiful," replied Jamie, and his eyes expressed the longing that was in his heart.

"Ten bob," said the man.

Just then two young children rushed up, exclaiming their delight at the pups in the basket, with their parents close behind them.

"Lovely dogs," said the man. "Best friend in the world. House trained, every one," and he began pushing puppies into the children's arms, smiling cheerfully as he expounded their virtues. Jamie, his hand still clutching his seven and sixpence halfpenny, unobtrusively slipped away.

For some time after that Jamie did not look at the dogs. He forced his way through the crowds, first on the pavement, then in the roadway, shuffling through wet newspapers, dodging below elbows, twisting around stalls, and when it seemed absolutely impossible to push through the seething mass of humanity he climbed over the wall on to a cleared bombed site and breathed freely for a moment or two.

Several boys were playing there, another was sorting through a pile of old comics he had just bought, two more were kicking a battered basket between goalposts indicated by their coats. Jamie watched them unseeingly. He was thinking of the dogs and the money in his pocket. His hand was hot and itchy now, clinging to the coins for so long, so he removed it from his pocket and rubbed it against his trousers. Even now he didn't have enough to buy a dog. Why were they so expensive?

Bitterly he kicked at a stone. He leaned his elbows on the wall and stared at the people beyond it, watching their faces, watching their hands as they pulled out silver and notes in exchange for the things they had bought.

Six suffocating goldfish in a jam jar. Three bob. Three angel fish in lukewarm water. Five and sixpence. A white mouse in a tiny cardboard box. Half a crown. Everybody was buying things, from battered radio sets to parakeets;

from jellied eels to jerseys; canaries, comics, and kittens. Tortoises and tiger barbs; pigeons and playing cards, and the smell of rabbits was mingled with the bittersweet smell of frying apple fritters.

That morning Jamie saw almost everything he could ever hope to see.

He saw a man juggling miraculously with a china tea service, every moment expecting the plates to crash to the pavement. He pitied the tortoises piled like small pyramids in yellow baskets, tucked under stalls laden with aquariums and accessories. He wondered if the tortoises could breathe, but at half a crown each he supposed that their owners hardly considered them much of a loss if they couldn't, otherwise they would have treated them less cruelly.

He watched with staring eyes while goldfish swam desperately out of reach of a determined net, wriggling, twisting, gliding, turning, caught at last. From net to jam jar, held up to be examined by all and sundry, with two drooping companions gasping for oxygen.

"Half a dollar, half a dollar," and the jar spun around in competent fingers. No one wanted them.

"Here," said the man. "Tell you what I'll do."

He didn't tell them, he showed them. He picked up another jam jar, also containing three goldfish. He poured those three in with the others.

"Three and six. Who'll give me three and six? Look here," he appealed to the crowd. "Half a dollar for three, three and six for six. What more can you ask? Look here."

He fished out six more from his large, murky aquarium. "Three and six," he said. Then six more. A man held up his hand.

"Right you are, sir. Three and sixpence."

Someone else wanted them. Business was warming up. Jamie wandered away. He wasn't really interested in fish. He had almost reached the end of the main body of the market. From here on it was mostly clothes for sale or goldfish. There were some rabbits on a barrow, packed so tightly into a couple of wire cages that they climbed over each other and stuck their claws into one another's faces.

"They can't move," cried Jamie in protest to the man in charge.

"You buying one?" he replied. "No? Well, hoppit."

II

Jamie spent two hours in Club Row. He was both repelled and enchanted by the things he saw; envious of the boys who sold old comics, records, and books; angry at the helplessness of the captive creatures—the bedraggled birds looking morose and sickly in their tiny cages, packed six or eight on a perch; the wild-eyed rabbits; the shivering hamsters. And when he had seen nearly everything he began the return journey to the part where the dogs were sold.

He did not hurry and neither did he find it so difficult to move. It was almost twelve-thirty and the crowds were not so thick. A slight rain caused the stallholders to start covering up their perishable goods. A mischievous wind caused the comic venders to search hastily for bricks while the birds cringed closer together in their cages and one or two undaunted spirits chirped bravely as they clung to the wire bars. Pigeons cooed, people argued, someone else gave racing tips, but Jamie stopped noticing most of these things because depression was creeping slowly over him.

Fighting his way through the crowds, seeing everything for the first time, standing in awe and pity, forgetting the reason for his being there, were emotions enough to keep him fully occupied. But now, on the way back, he had seen everything, the winds and rain were cold, the people were dispersing. He felt miserable.

His mind was full of the struggling or defeated animals, the bartering over their helpless bodies, the dirt, the dampness, and the smells. He passed the jellied eel stall, feeling sick, and suddenly he found himself running; running back to the dogs that smelled sweet, where the bartering was not so fierce nor the crowds so thick; where he hoped to find his future companion.

He pulled his jacket closer around him, for by now the gusty wind had increased in cold and power. The slight rain was falling more heavily and the clouds in the sky were gathering into large black islands. One or two stallholders were beginning to pack up; kittens into baskets, one, two, three. Perhaps till next week, thought Jamie.

There were only two nice Alsatians left. They had been five pounds before. Now they were three pounds ten. Jamie eyed them enviously. They were big dogs, even at that age, with huge round paws and floppy ears, lolling tongues, and innocent eyes. Jamie grinned as he watched them, pawing halfheartedly at each other in boredom, yawning and shaking their heads as the rain splashed down. His depression began to fade. How could he be anything but happy watching these lovely creatures?

Someone else was packing up and steady streams of people were making their way to the bus stop, laden with purchases of one kind or another, reminding Jamie that if he did not buy a dog soon it would be too late. Where was the man with the mongrels? If they were ten shillings before they might be down to seven and six by now.

The man was still there with his mongrels, but he had only four left. Among them was one that Jamie had held. He stroked its back with one finger and smiled when it turned on to its back, waving its paws in the air.

"How much is he?" Jamie asked the man.

"How much you got?" he replied.

"Five shillings," said Jamie.

"Go on with you. You're wasting my time."

"Seven and six?"

"Ten bob," said the man. "Not a penny less. It's cost me that much to feed him."

"I haven't got ten bob," said Jamie.

"Then there's nothing you can buy from me."

"But if you don't sell him this week it'll cost you more to save him till next time," argued Jamie, not yet defeated.

"You're not my only customer, sonny. I'd be doing you a favor at ten bob."

Jamie stared at him, disbelief in his eyes. He felt sure this pup was going to be his. Surely the man would go lower. His lip trembled and he clenched his fist over the money in his pocket.

"I haven't got ten bob," he said again.

"Then you're unlucky," said the man.

Jamie turned away without looking again at the dog. He hunched his shoulders, feeling the wind bitterly, feeling a lump in his throat. He shuffled along the pavement, kicking at a broken cardboard box. He stopped at the next stall where two corgis lay tucked into each other, fast asleep.

"Twenty-five bob," said the man, and Jamie shook his head.

The next stall was empty and Jamie stared down at the straw, which grew darker as he watched the rain fall down upon it. Then he heard a long, doleful whine and looked up anxiously, feeling the pain in the cry because it expressed so fully the feelings within himself.

There was an old man standing in the middle of the road. He had two notes in his hand and looked down at them, turning them over and over as if not recognizing them as such. He had just sold his dog to someone else and Jamie watched the dog with pity.

It must have been about five years old, a not very handsome boxer. Jamie remembered having seen him with the old man when he first arrived and he had wondered then why the man just stood there, the dog at his feet lying in the damp roadway.

He had sold his dog just now; sold him to a complete stranger. Handed him over, just like that, as if he were selling an ornament or an unwanted overcoat. Jamie could not believe in such treachery, and neither could the dog.

He kept turning back, uttering that doleful whine. He had sat all morning in the rain at his master's feet, pressed against his legs, and now he pulled back against the man who held him, trying to reach his master, not knowing that he had been discarded.

His new owner did not seem to understand what was the matter. He pulled him along impatiently, anxious to get out of the rain no doubt. The dog refused to go. He was big and strong. He turned and strained toward his master, who would not look in his direction but still stared at the money in his hands.

The dog stood on his hind legs, jaws gaping because the collar around his throat was half choking him, pawing the air with his front legs and whining desperately. But when his master would not turn around he seemed to realize what had happened, for he dropped to all fours again and miserably followed in the wake of the man who held his lead.

After that Jamie wanted to go home. He was sick of the market. He didn't want to buy a dog, not one of these anyway. And as he stood in the line waiting for the bus his thoughts took up their familiar train. He knew then that there was only one dog he really wanted, the one dog he could never have, and his love for Silver Streak grew stronger.

The greyhound was part of his life, even though he could never possess him. So Jamie sat sadly on the bus going home, wanting deeply but glad that he had not bought a dog.

He only wanted Silver.

6

The Five-pound Note

I

Jamie's heart was glad when he ran down the street to the house where the old man lived but his footsteps slowed as he neared it for there was a boy sitting on the doorstep, a boy he had never seen before. He was no more than seven or eight years old, with curly black hair and freckled face. There was a small ginger kitten struggling frantically in his lap while the boy was industriously engaged in pushing stones into its ears.

"You mustn't do that!" exclaimed Jamie.

"Why not?" retorted the boy. "It's my kitten."

"Leave it alone. You're hurting it," and Jamie tried to drag the kitten away.

The boy resisted for a minute or two, then Jamie pushed him hard so that he fell backwards on the steps. He began to scream, although Jamie knew that he couldn't possibly be hurt.

"I'll tell my mum about you," he threatened between screams. "Just you wait."

"And I'll tell her what you were doing with the kitten."

"It's mine. I'll do what I like."

Very soon the door opened and a woman appeared. She looked at the boy on the step and she glared at Jamie who still held the kitten in his arms.

"What's going on? What've you been up to?" she said, and Jamie answered before the other boy could get a word in.

"He was putting stones in the kitten's ears and I told him not to."

"Well, it's none of your business. And you stop your crying, Tommy. You're not hurt. I've told you half a dozen times to leave that kitten alone. Come on in," and she grabbed him by the shoulders, dragged him indoors, and slammed the door.

Jamie sat on the doorstep for a minute or two, placing the kitten beside him and tenderly stroking it. The little creature knew that the boy meant no harm and did not cringe away. She had a thin, mournful face and Jamie was not surprised. Fancy belonging to a boy like that! He thought how unfair it was that someone who was cruel should own an animal while he, who loved them, should be denied. He examined her ears, but she must have managed to shake the stones out for, apart from being a bit dusty, they were all right.

"Well, puss, I can't play with you all day. I've got other things to do," he said, and he got up and banged on the door.

While he waited for the old man to come down the kitten rubbed herself round his legs, purring softly and occasionally mewing. Jamie smiled, full of contentment, thinking that in a few minutes he and Silver would be on their way to the park together. He supposed it was better to have a dog to take out than have no dog at all and now he had seven shillings left in his savings which made him feel very rich.

He peered through the glass panel at the side of the door. The old man was a long time coming down. He knocked again and he played with the kitten while waiting. At last the old man opened the door but there was that same strange, distant expression in his eyes that Jamie had seen two or three times before. The old man said nothing as he let the boy in, slowly following him up the stairs, breathing heavily.

When they reached the old man's room Jamie was surprised to see that it looked more tidy than usual.

"I've been cleaning up a bit," said the old man by way of explanation. "You see, I shan't be here much longer."

Jamie's heart seemed to beat faster at the words. Supposing he moved a long way away and he were never to see Silver again? He waited to hear more.

"Sit down, Jamie lad. I've got something to tell

you. I've just made a cup of tea so pour yourself one
if you like."

Now Jamie knew that something was wrong. The
old man gave a deep sigh and sank into his armchair
with a gesture of despair. Jamie forgot about the tea.

"What's the matter? Can I help?" he begged. "Is
it about Silver?"

The questions rushed out. He stared anxiously at the
old man, impatient to hear what he had to say. But
already he knew it was about Silver and a sick feeling
had come to his stomach as he waited.

"It's like this, laddie. I've got to move away from
here. Can't afford the rent on my old-age pension and
I'm three weeks behind already. The landlady's been
very good to me, hasn't complained much, but she
has to make a living, too, and can't afford to keep
an old man like me out of charity. So I'm going to
one of them homes for old people. Can't say as I
like the idea much but haven't got any choice. Got
to live somewhere. Can't live in the street."

"But what about Silver?" cried Jamie, not caring
that he had expressed no sympathy for the old man's
state.

"That's just it. Silver."

He lingered over the name of his dog and the
greyhound drew near to him, looking up at him with
anxiety also. He could sense that something was amiss
and felt the sadness of his master.

"I can't take Silver with me, laddie. They don't
allow dogs in the home. So he's got to stay behind."

"What are you going to do with him then?"

"Well, as I told you, I'm three weeks behind with the rent and, as the landlady knows I've got no money, she says I can give the dog to her little boy and she won't say no more."

"What little boy's that?"

"Oh, some little chap. About eight. Perhaps you've seen him."

"Has he got a kitten?"

"That's the one. Lives downstairs. I don't like him very much, but, there, what can I do? I owe his mother four pounds ten."

"But you can't do that!" exclaimed Jamie. "You just can't. Silver would hate it. He'd miss you so much and I wouldn't be able to take him out any more. And he's cruel, that boy. I've just seen him. He was pushing stones in the kitten's ears. Please, mister. You can't give Silver to him."

"What else can I do, Jamie? I've got no choice. It's settled."

There were tears in Jamie's eyes, but the old man was too shortsighted to see them. There was a long silence. Jamie was thinking of how he had planned to desert Silver and buy a dog of his own, and now, as if punishment for his intended treachery, Silver was was to be taken away from him. The old man was remembering all the days and years he had spent with only his dog for company. He too was crying, but there were no tears for him. He had learned long ago to control his tears. Only his heart wept.

He sighed. "Well, Jamie, there it is. That's how it goes. I shall miss the old dog and no doubt he'll miss us both. Perhaps you can make friends with the little boy and both go out with Silver."

"Never," retorted Jamie. "He's horrible and cruel and I don't know how you could dream of leaving Silver with him. Please don't do it."

"Jamie, I . . ."

"I'll find the money. Four pounds ten, you said. I'll get it and you can sell Silver to me. Will you do that? Will you wait just a little? I'll get the money, I know I will."

"But how?"

"Don't worry about that. I'll get it. I'll buy Silver. Please don't give him to that boy, that's all."

From that day Jamie's troubles began.

II

Jamie had no idea where he could get such a sum of money. A hundred pounds would have been just as easy to obtain. He had seven shillings, Cora had about two shillings, and neither of them was to have a birthday for a long time. He knew it would be hopeless to ask his parents and, anyway, they said he could not have a dog.

Jamie did not consider this last at all. He felt sure that if he went home with the dog his mother would say yes, especially once she had seen what a lovely creature Silver was. But the thoughts of the money haunted him. The old man had only a week left in his room before he went to the home and if he didn't have the money by then it would be too late.

All week long at school Jamie considered the problem. No one noticed his preoccupation. Jamie was always silent in class and completely ignored by both pupils and teachers. He stared out of the window, watching rain drizzling down the panes, screwing up his eyes against the occasional glare of sunshine, and when Friday came he still had not solved the problem. The bell rang for lunch and the others rushed out, nearly knocking the teacher over, but Jamie sat where he was, too numbed with misery as he thought of the morrow to even realize that morning school was over.

He was not entirely alone. There was one other person in the room. Hilliard. He stared in silence at Jamie for several minutes then sauntered over to him and sat on his desk.

"What's the matter, Vince?"

Jamie looked up. No one had ever called him Vince before. It sounded friendly and rather grown-up.

"Well? That Silverman again? Has he been bothering you?"

"No, it's not him. It's something else."

"Well, what is it? I'm asking you. What is it?"

Jamie sighed. He looked down at the desk lid which was inscribed with many scrawled initials, stained with blobs of ink, and mostly occupied by Hilliard's leg.

"You can't help me. No one can help me. And tomorrow it's too late."

"How do you know I can't help you if you don't tell me what it is?"

Jamie looked at the older boy again. He seemed friendly and anxious to help and Jamie did not know why. But he was longing to tell someone of his troubles and Hilliard was the only one eager to hear. He began telling him the whole story from when he had first seen the greyhound right up to the present, finishing, "And if I don't have the money by tomorrow the old man is going to give Silver away and I'll never see him again."

"So all you want is four pounds ten. Why didn't you say so before instead of giving me all this rigmarole? Anyone would think you were asking for the world instead of only four pounds ten."

"It is to me. I've never had that much money in my life."

"Well, you're only a kid. Look."

Hilliard put his hand inside his jacket pocket and casually pulled out a wad of notes. Jamie's eyes grew bigger as he nonchalantly slung them on the desk. They fell in scattered array, some of them on the floor.

"Gosh! Crikey!"

It was all Jamie could say.

"How much do you want?" said Hilliard. "Is this okay?"

He picked up a grubby piece of white paper. It was a five-pound note.

"Where did you get all this money from?" exclaimed Jamie.

"Now you're asking questions. Just take this fiver and the dog's yours."

"But, Hilliard, I can't. How can I pay you back? I only get sixpence a week."

"Never you mind about that. Just take the money.

Maybe you'll be able to do a little job for me one day, then we'll be quits."

He smiled at Jamie, but Jamie was too filled with doubt, amazement, and delight to smile back. He knew it was wrong to take the money, but his longing to possess Silver and keep him from the other boy was too great to be denied.

"Gosh, thanks, Hilliard. Are you sure?"

"Look, kid, take it and do what you like with it. I've got plenty more. My old man's just won the pools."

Almost reverently Jamie took the five-pound note, folded it, and put it in his trouser pocket. His heart leaped with excitement and he could hardly wait for school to be over for the day. He would go this very night to the old man and buy Silver from him. This very night Silver would be his.

III

Jamie was filled with joy and apprehension as he took the dog from the old man, said goodbye to him for the last time, and then set off for home. It was wonderful to walk through the streets with Silver, knowing that at long last the greyhound was his.

He grinned with delight, watching the shadows of the two of them advancing along the pavement, realizing that from now on when he walked the streets it would always be with Silver at his side. But his grin faded when he thought of the opposition he was bound to face when he reached home. What would his mother say? Would she relent when she saw what a wonderful dog Silver was and how much he loved him?

He decided that it would be best not to tell her about the five pounds and he hastily pushed thoughts of the loan to the back of his mind. That was a worry he was not prepared to consider at the moment.

It was a lovely evening. The sun was warm, lingering long over the half-deserted streets and throwing shadows of lampposts and railings across the pavements and roadways. Jamie felt like dancing and he constantly paused to pat his dog, saying his name over and over again.

"Silver, my Silver. Silver. You're mine now."

The greyhound looked up at Jamie with puzzlement expressed in his eyes. There was a new delight in the boy's voice which he had not heard before. Silver had sensed all week that something was wrong, that something different was going to happen. His master had been sad, Jamie had been sad. He could not understand why, but he trusted Jamie and followed even though he knew that things were different now.

When Jamie came to his house he hesitated before going up the stairs. He remembered how emphatically his mother had told him that he could not have a dog and he was afraid again. The sinking feeling, against which he had been striving for some time, returned and for a few minutes he sat on the doorstep with his dog, fondling his ears, before plucking up hope and courage enough to push open the door.

He went slowly up the stairs, holding Silver by the

collar. The greyhound sensed his apprehension and whined.

"Ssh!" said Jamie softly, not wanting his mother to hear, although he knew that he must confront her with Silver in a moment or two.

"Quiet, Silver boy. Be good. You've got to make a good impression."

He halted outside Mr. Doherty's flat and took a deep breath. It wasn't the stairs that took his breath away but his apprehension. With every new step his dread became greater. He still felt sure that his mother would say no. The staircase was dark and silent and Jamie's footsteps sounded so loudly that he felt sure the whole house must hear them.

Then he plucked up courage. Only ten stairs remained to his own door. He took Silver's collar more firmly, hurried up, and opened the door as naturally as he could. His mother, Cora, and Leah all turned to look at him as he entered.

"Jamie!" exclaimed Mrs. Vincent. "Where on earth have you been?"

Then she saw the dog.

"And where did you get that dog? Jamie, what have you been up to? We had tea about an hour ago."

"Hello, Mum. I've been to see a friend of mine. He gave me his dog because he can't keep him any more and he didn't have anyone to give him to but me."

"You must take it back, Jamie. We can't keep it. I told you before you couldn't have a dog. Such a great big thing too. Really, Jamie, you're a very naughty boy."

"But Mum . . ."

"Take the dog back, Jamie. We can't keep it here," and Jamie knew by her tone that she meant what she said.

7

The Cellar

I

Jamie stared at his mother incredulously. He had expected her to be angry, had expected her to shout at him, perhaps even hit him, but he had not really expected her to say, "Take the dog back."

There was a long, pregnant silence between them. Silver sensed that he was the cause of the argument and he slunk beneath the table, his head on his paws, his eyes staring first at Jamie and then at Mrs. Vincent, troubled and afraid.

"Mum, I can't take him back."

"Why not? You do just what I tell you, Jamie, and don't argue."

"But I've bought him. Paid for him. He's mine."

"Then you must get the money back. Oh, I don't care if you get the money or not. Just get rid of the dog. We can't have him here."

"Mum, Mum!" Jamie's voice was choked with pleading. "Please don't send him away. I can't bear it if you send him away."

"Don't be silly, Jamie. Of course you can bear it. You'll get over it in a day or two."

"But I love him, Mum."

Tears rolled down his cheeks as he realized the hopelessness of his plea. His mother was determined and very angry. He could not understand why she was so angry, why she was so determined to get rid of the dog. Did she hate him, not want him to be happy? Why didn't she want him to have a dog? He began to cry with loud, uncontrollable sobs. He sat down in a chair, pressed his hands over his face, and really cried. Cora stared with amazement. So did his mother.

"Stop it, Jamie. Stop it."

She put her arms around him consolingly, but he tore himself away.

"Jamie, it's impossible to love a dog that much."

"Why?"

"You mustn't. It'll bring you nothing but trouble."

"How do you know? How do you know? Oh, Mum, I love him and I want him."

"Don't, Jamie, don't. Like him but don't love him. Take him back where he comes from." She relented a little and spoke more softly. "Please, Jamie. Try to understand. We can't have him here."

Jamie stopped crying. His mother was adamant. His hope had died and he was too empty now to cry. Silver must go, where to he did not know, his mother did not care, but he couldn't stay at home with them. He looked up at his mother, unashamed of his tear-stained face, and unable to control the sneer of hatred on his lips.

"Jamie!" she cried, astonished. "Don't look at me like that. What's the matter?"

He wanted to say something to really hurt her as she had hurt him, but he could think of nothing hard or cruel enough. The more he tried to think, the less clear his mind became and the sneer in his eyes and on his lips grew more pronounced.

"You can't have the dog, Jamie, so stop loving him. Forget him. Take him back where he belongs. I told you before you couldn't have a dog."

"I hate you," said Jamie suddenly. "I hate you. You don't know nothing about love. You don't love me. Well, I don't love you neither. I hate you."

"Jamie! What are you saying?"

"I said I hate you."

Then his mother became very angry again. She was not sorry for him any more. Even Cora was against him. He could see that from the way she looked at him.

"You'll take that dog back right this minute if you know what's good for you," Mrs. Vincent commanded. "It's a good job your father isn't here. Go on. Take it back and don't come home till you've got rid of it."

She strode to the door and opened it wide, pointing down the stairs.

"Go on, now. Take him back. And let's have no more of it."

Jamie could see that she was trembling and he was afraid. He didn't really mean what he had said to her, but he could not tell her that now. She would not let him keep Silver and she was too angry even to listen to him. Silently he crawled under the table and took hold of the dog's collar.

"Come on, boy," he said. "Nobody wants us here. Let's go somewhere else. Come on."

Silver reluctantly followed him, still cringing, sensing the tense atmosphere and the unhappiness of his new master. Jamie looked up at his mother as he passed her on his way down the stairs but there was no softening in her face. It was hard and angry and yet somehow troubled with other emotions. Jamie had never seen his mother like this before. He wanted to fling his arms around her and sob, and have her pat his shoulder and rub his hair, but she looked too cold so he didn't.

He went down the stairs with Silver and silently shut the front door behind him. The light of day was already beginning to fade and there was an orange glow behind the chimney pots of the houses opposite. It was chilly and he pulled his jacket closer to him. He dragged the piece of string from his pocket and bent to tie it to Silver's collar. The dog looked at him mournfully. Perhaps he was missing the old man or perhaps he knew that Jamie was sad.

"Please don't, Silver. Don't look at me like that. Love me, boy. Trust me. I'll find you somewhere to live. You belong to me now and I'll look after you."

But where could he take him if not home? He couldn't take him back to the old man. There was no one who could help him. For the first time in his life Jamie felt utterly alone and the damp, pointed muzzle pressing into the palm of his hand for once did not comfort him.

II

Jamie wandered up and down the streets for what seemed ages, going nowhere in particular, hardly even considering his predicament. Not for one second had he any intention of renouncing Silver but further than that he did not think.

He found himself walking along beside a low brick

wall, probably recently constructed for the bricks were very clean. There was nothing on the other side, which dropped away to a cleared bombed site, except a view of the backs of the houses on the next street. There was a gate at the end of the wall, next to an occupied house, and it was partially open. He halted when he reached the gate and, because he had nothing else to do, he decided to explore.

Jamie went slowly down the steps, wondering if they were safe. His mother was constantly warning him against playing on bombed sites, telling him of the dangers of loose brickwork and rotting floorboards, but, filled with defiance, Jamie was glad to be doing something his mother would not permit.

It seemed strange to walk down the area steps of a house that wasn't there and, in the increasing gloom of twilight, Jamie felt like an intruder. He was glad that it was growing dark. No one would be able to see him and he could be alone with his dog.

He stared about for a few minutes when he reached the last step before moving to explore, looking up at the high walls on either side of him which still traced out dusty patterns of fireplaces and wallpaper, stairways and cupboards, while the moonlight gleamed on discolored bath tiles that still remained high up on one of the walls. Ten years ago three large houses had occupied this desolate spot but all that remained to tell of their one-time existence was the scarred walls of the first and last houses and the one area stairway.

The site had long been cleared of debris and the flat, solid squares of stone, which had once been basement floors, glistened damply where they were not covered with dust. Against each wall were straggling heaps of discolored bricks and rubble, sprouting grass and weeds, while one wall was shored by strong beams of timber set obliquely against it, painted with creosote.

There were shadows everywhere, strange in shape. There were cardboard boxes, sodden with rainwater; two rusty, twisted milk crates; old shoes; broken bottles glinting in the half-light thrown by the street lamps up on the pavement.

Then Jamie became aware of the cellars. Gaping black holes, they stretched in long tunnels under the street and looked like caverns in a hillside. In the semi-darkness Jamie hesitated before exploring them fully, wondering what he might find within them. Then he felt Silver's damp nose pressing against his leg, the warm tongue worming its way between his fingers, and he was reassured.

"Come on, boy," he said softly. "Let's see what's inside."

The first cellar contained nothing but rubbish. It was black and evil-smelling. Jamie's shoulder accidentally brushed against the wall and, feeling the cold wetness of the brickwork with his hands, he shuddered involuntarily. Silver seemed unperturbed by the darkness. He padded backwards and forwards, sniffing inquiringly into boxes and newspapers, acting like an ambitious pup instead of as the old dog that he was.

The second cellar was no more exciting than the first and Jamie wondered how all the rubbish came to be there. He wondered if they were visited by anyone in particular, but he could not imagine why they should be. While he picked up this and examined that, he became accustomed to the gloom and dankness, engrossed in his explorations.

The doorway to the third cellar was almost impassable, it being piled high with bricks and rubbish in general. But Jamie was determined to explore it and, with some difficulty, climbed over the heap, slipping and sliding but gaining entrance. It was very dark in the third cellar, with very little air, and Jamie knew that no one had been here for a long time. There was hardly any rubbish at all scattered over the earthen floor, while in one corner was a firmly fixed shelf with three old paint tins on it.

He also made another discovery. The third cellar led directly into the fourth by way of a hole in the wall, not very wide or high but large enough for a boy of Jamie's stature to squeeze through. In the fourth cellar, which was open to the air, was a huge pile of sand, very wet but clean, and Jamie guessed that it had not been there for long.

By this time it was too dark to see what the other cellars might contain, so Jamie decided to explore no farther. His own problems, which he had forgotten in the eagerness of discovery, were pushing themselves uppermost again and overwhelming him. It was getting late. He had to go home soon and still he had not decided what to do with Silver.

"Silver. My beautiful dog. Silver," said Jamie, and the old greyhound came nuzzling up to him, warming his cold legs with the heat of his body, warming his heart with his closeness.

Jamie sat down on an old beer crate and stroked Silver softly around the throat. His mind was a blank. Weary with thinking, he could think no more. He didn't know what to do with Silver. All he knew was that Silver belonged to him now and that he could not give him up.

Jamie shivered. It was cold in the cellar. He wondered if tramps ever came to this place to sleep. Perhaps they did when it was raining and they had nowhere else to go. Slowly an idea came to him. He could keep Silver in one of these cellars. Make a warm little nest for him, bring him food every day, come to see him in every spare moment. No one would ever know. But he would have to keep him tied up for fear that he might wander away and get lost or be run over. He did not like the idea very much, leaving Silver all alone in the cold, dark dampness, but, as far as he could see, there was no alternative.

But which was the driest, warmest, and most sheltered of the cellars? Of those he had explored the third seemed the obvious choice.

Ideas came swiftly now and he sprang up from the crate, intending to waste no time because he had very little left. He collected up all the old crates and boxes, the soggy bundles of newspapers, the rags and tatters, both within the cellars and without, throwing them into a jumbled heap through the hole in the wall that connected cellars three and four. He intended to make a kind of kennel for his dog to keep out the drafts and dampness and, although his materials were primitive, at least they were in plentiful supply.

Jamie worked industriously, watched with curiosity by Silver. He filled the boxes with newspaper, made a platform from an old door raised from the earth by bricks, and placed the paper-stuffed boxes all around it. He wished he could find something dry for Silver to lie on, but that was beyond the scope of those moss-coated cellars under the street. So Jamie, not caring what his mother might say, decided to spread his jacket over the door in the hope that it would give Silver both warmth and contentment.

All he needed to do now was find something secure to which he could tie his dog. There was nothing, but Jamie was not defeated. He could block up the connecting hole between the cellars and Silver would not be able to escape—he hoped!

At last all was complete. Jamie had done everything toward his dog's comfort that he could think of and now it was time to go home. He settled Silver on his coat on the platform and fondled him gently.

Silver did not want to stay there. He did not like the dark, cold corner and could not understand the preparations that Jamie had made for him.

"Be a good boy. I'll be here first thing tomorrow with some food," Jamie promised him. "Don't worry, Silver. I'm not leaving you for good. I'll be back," and he spoke constantly to the restless, puzzled greyhound, trying to calm him, trying to convince himself that all would be well.

It was not easy, and as the minutes fled by Jamie could not tear himself from his dog. He sat beside him on the door, stroking and talking, and his sadness came back because he could not have Silver at home.

Everything was going wrong. Why couldn't things go

as he had planned in his dreams? Why couldn't his mother relent? But Jamie was beginning to learn that only in dreams did things turn out the way you wanted them to. He was facing reality for the first time and he was not prepared to meet it.

Already to keep Silver he had borrowed money that he could never repay. He had defied his mother and hurt her deeply. He was provoking more trouble at home by staying out so late. He would have to tell lies when he returned. But, above all, he was leaving Silver alone, alone in a black, damp cellar, with no warmth or food or water, gaining nothing by all that he had done so far.

Jamie sighed, feeling heavy with dread and despair. He was weary too, weary of thinking and crying and hurting, weary of everything but Silver. There seemed to be no way out of his predicament. He was involving himself more and more, beginning a web from which there was no escape, and he tried to shake away the probing doubts within him, too tired to answer or explain them.

At last he slowly rose, patting Silver once more and kissing his silky skull.

"Be a good boy," he said. "I'll come back tomorrow," and by his tone and manner the dog knew that Jamie would not permit him to follow.

From his corner on the platform he watched Jamie block up the hole with wood and crates and rubble and, when he could no longer see him, he heard his footsteps fade away.

A slow whine rose to Silver's throat, ending in a short yelp as he jumped up and ran to the place where the hole

had been. Jamie's scent lingered strongly there and eagerly Silver inhaled it, whimpering and scratching all the while. But he knew that Jamie meant him to stay, although he could not understand the reason for it.

Dejectedly he returned to the platform on which Jamie had left his jacket. Slowly Silver sniffed it over, nuzzling through the sleeves and pockets, smelling Jamie in every fold. He whimpered again, lonely and cold, and it was a long time before the blackness of the cellar merged with the blackness of sleep.

III

Jamie went slowly home, shivering involuntarily now and then because he was cold without his jacket.

The streets near home were almost deserted, for it was nearly eleven o'clock. He could hear the hum of traffic on the main road, a background to the shuffle of his lonely feet on the pavement, but it seemed a long way off.

He was dreading going home, remembering the things he had said, remembering his mother's face. But, in a way, he was glad too. He was more lonely now than he had ever been—trapped on an island of his own creation —and in the gathering darkness of his confusion his love for Silver offered him the only gleam of light.

8

First Problems

I

Mrs. Vincent realized that she had been rather hard on Jamie. She had not meant to be so harsh, but she had not understood the extent of Jamie's love for the scruffy old dog he had brought home. It wasn't that she disliked dogs or didn't want Jamie to have one. It was just that they couldn't afford to keep a dog, as she had told him.

She waited anxiously for Jamie to come home and as the hours passed she became worried. He had eaten nothing since lunchtime at school and now it was ten o'clock. Cora had been in bed for an hour and was asleep. Mr. Vincent was working until midnight and therefore Jamie's mother was alone with her worries.

She decided that when Jamie came home she would be nice to him. She would talk calmly and explain again why he could not keep a dog. Poor Jamie. He was an affectionate boy and she had been deeply shocked by his bitter words. They rang in her mind again and again and she could not forget them. Did he love the dog so much that he could turn against her and utter such terrible words?

She cleared the table, picked up the scattered toys from the floor, washed the crockery, and constantly looked at the clock. She had put Jamie's dinner in the oven to keep warm, but now it had dried up and was hardly eatable. She decided to cook him something fresh when he returned. But where was he? When would he come back? The ticking of the clock sounded very loud in her ears and she wished she had someone to talk to.

At last she heard footsteps on the stairs. It must be Jamie. She ran to the door to open it for him and the glow which spread down the dark staircase illuminated his solitary figure as he came slowly toward her.

"Jamie!" she exclaimed. "Where have you been! I've been so worried about you."

Jamie did not reply. He was no longer angry with his mother, but he was too tired and miserable to care.

"Come on in quickly, Jamie. You must be tired—and hungry. You sit down at the table and I'll cook you something. Do you want a cup of hot milk or cocoa?"

"I'm not hungry," said Jamie listlessly.

"You must be. Come on, sit yourself down."

She could see that his jacket was missing, but made no comment, determined to be kind to him and make him repent. She did not mention the dog either, fearing his reaction to any questions concerning Silver, but bustled about preparing him food and something to drink.

Jamie sat at the table and watched his mother. He thought of Silver in the cellar and hoped that he would be all right. He no longer hated his mother for saying that he could not keep his dog. Silver had a home now. Silver was still his and he suddenly felt ashamed of himself, wishing that he had never made his mother unhappy.

Mrs. Vincent was frying bacon and eggs for him and the smell wafted to him from the little kitchen, giving him some appetite after all. He watched her closely, all her movements, seeing her for the first time as a person as well as a mother. She was thin and small, with gray eyes like Jamie's but dark hair like Cora's, which was never very tidy. Her clothes were never smart because she could rarely afford to buy new things for herself and wore the same dresses and skirts year after year. But to Jamie she was the most beautiful mother in the world and he suddenly jumped up from the table and rushed into the kitchen, crying one word.

"Mum."

He pressed close against her and she put her arms around him. Jamie was crying, but his mother was smiling as she held him tightly. They both knew that their quarrel was over and that everything would be all right between them again.

By the time Mr. Vincent had come home from work that night it was very late and Jamie was asleep in the room he shared with his two sisters. He was exhausted and slept without dreaming, but his parents sat talking for some time, discussing him mostly, for Mrs. Vincent lost no time in telling her husband what had happened that evening.

"Poor kid," said Jamie's father. "I used to want a dog when I was his age but could never have one. Made do with rats instead. But it's not the same. Rats are funny things."

"Well, don't tell Jamie about them or he'll be wanting some and I couldn't stand rats about the place, especially with the baby. They might get out and bite her."

Mr. Vincent laughed. He was a cheerful man, rarely concerned with anything beyond his family and his work, and the face above the navy, white-cuffed driver's uniform was round and happy. He wasn't fat, but he certainly was not thin, and he blamed his figure on his job, saying that sitting behind a wheel all day did not give him a chance to keep his waist in trim.

"The fact is, Eve," he continued, "Jamie might be able to have his dog after all. Not yet, of course, and not here. But when I was having a cuppa in the café this evening I heard a couple of blokes talking about these new factories going up in the country, Harlow and Stevenage and places like that. It seems that if you get a job with them there's a chance of getting a house too. Now, if I could get a driving job with one of them places and we got a home in the country, Jamie could have his dog, a great big one if he wanted it."

"It sounds a lovely idea," replied Jamie's mother. "But I shan't say anything to Jamie. You know how he sets his heart on things. He's got rid of the dog now so it's best not to go upsetting him again. Let's wait till you've got the job before we say anything. But it would be lovely."

They talked on for a while, for the idea of a home in the country and a dog for Jamie was pleasant to both of them.

II

From then on Jamie had some fine times with Silver. The early summer evenings grew longer and lighter and they were able to spend a couple of hours in the park together nearly every night, strolling around the Serpentine, sitting under the trees, watching those who came and went. The dogs, the children, the old ladies, the young lovers, the students with their books and papers, the occasional artist and horseman.

Jamie was not lonely any more and neither was Silver. Sometimes Jamie talked lengthily to his dog and at other times he would sit silently with him, not needing to speak, feeling the warmth of his presence, filled with contentment by the very knowledge that the greyhound was his completely—not just a possession, but a living, breathing, warm-blooded creature who gave Jamie love and company; who trusted him as he had never been trusted; who gave him a feeling of importance and surrounded him with security from the ache of loneliness which he had known before Silver became his dog.

Jamie was not ambitious for Silver as many boys are for their dogs. He did not want him to win prizes in shows, to be bigger, stronger, or more beautiful than any other dog, to outpace or outfight the bully dogs. All he wanted him to be was his dog alone, loving him and trusting him, a friend. And Jamie knew he was that.

He sometimes wondered if Silver missed the old man. He never wondered if the old man missed his dog, selfishly forgetting that the greyhound had once brought happiness and companionship to another. But Silver had grown to look upon Jamie as a second master and he was content to be with the boy and, in a way, more happy. Jamie talked to him a lot and Silver liked that. The old man rarely spoke, except in an indistinct mumble, so that until Silver had met Jamie he had lived in a world of semi-silence, becoming dull and listless like his master.

Now he was younger. His eyes grew bright, his tail often wagged, and there was more spring in his steps these days. He no longer dutifully followed Jamie, nose close to the boy's left leg, but sometimes pranced ahead, or lingered behind sniffing some strange scent. When Jamie laughed and shouted to him Silver opened his mouth and wriggled his body with delight, his long tongue lolling out of his jaws. He sometimes jumped up at Jamie and even barked occasionally. He was altogether a different dog.

But he hated being left in the cellar throughout the long day and night. He would try to follow Jamie when the boy left him, whimpering and scrabbling at the rubble which barred his path, one day succeeding in escaping through the hole and chasing after Jamie with delight. From then on Jamie knew that he would have to tie Silver up or else he would lose him, so the next day he took a nail along to the cellar and banged it into the wall between the stones with a brick. It was a long nail and resisted Jamie's efforts to pull it out, therefore he knew it would be safe. To this he tethered Silver when he left him and the dog knew that Jamie did not want him to follow.

The nail was only the first of many things that Jamie took to the cellar. Week by week he made a little home in that place and spent every Saturday and Sunday there, cleaning it and making it more comfortable.

He found an old broom head, half rotten and evil-smelling, but with this he swept the floor of his cellar, afterwards spreading it with the soft clean sand piled in the fourth cellar. He made Silver's box more comfortable by keeping it well supplied with newspapers taken from home, and, as time passed and he felt more and more secure in this hiding place of his, he began to bring some of his treasures from home and keep them there.

Jamie's mother was curious when she saw things begin to disappear from the flat, wondering what her son was up to now. His model airplane, a flashlight, an old cracked vase all vanished and one day he asked her for the piece of coconut matting from the kitchen which she intended to throw away.

"Why? What do you want it for, Jamie?" she asked him.

"Well, you see I've got a secret hiding place. It's a sort of cellar and I like to go there to play. I wanted to make it more comfortable, that's all."

"And where is this secret hiding place?" Mrs. Vincent wanted to know next.

"Oh, around," was Jamie's vague reply. "Not far from here. On a bomb site."

"Jamie, what have I told you about playing on bomb sites?"

"It's not dangerous, Mum, honest it isn't. I wouldn't go there if it was. It's been cleared. Please don't say I can't go there."

"Well, all right. But be careful what you do, Jamie. Places can look safe but that doesn't mean they are."

She gave him the mat and two chipped cups as well.

"Have you got anything else to spare?" asked Jamie eagerly.

"Not at the moment. But I'll have a look around while you're out tonight. I suppose you'll be out again tonight. You're always out these days, Jamie."

"I go to my hideout, that's why," and he returned her questioning stare unblushingly.

Jamie took the matting and the cups gladly and one Saturday morning spent his weekly sixpence on candles and matches so that it would not be so dark in his cellar. He thought carefully about this expenditure, for now he was discovering that he needed far more than sixpence a week in order to keep his dog.

He had not realized how much it would cost to feed a dog of Silver's size, nor how much food Silver could eat. He looked so skinny, with ribs showing through his hide, that Jamie was under the impression that he ate very little. Luckily he had plenty of time to consider this problem, for he had about eighteen shillings in his possession now, ten left over from the five-pound note and the rest was his savings.

He bought bones from a butcher for threepence or fourpence, dog biscuits, cheap fish, and various canned foods. Silver wolfed his way through a packet of biscuits for one meal and the bones were not food at all, only something to nibble at as he whiled away the lonely hours.

Jamie was startled when he saw Silver eat, hurriedly working out how much it would cost him per week. When he added it up the total came to nine or ten shillings at least. He was shocked. No wonder the old man couldn't afford to keep him any longer. Ten shillings in one week! And his pocket money was sixpence. What could he do? If he kept all his dinner money as well it would only make four and threepence.

"Oh, Silver," he groaned, "I wish you were a bit smaller."

That night Jamie had a nightmare. He dreamed that he had forgotten all about Silver and that it was only by chance that, three or four weeks later, he found himself walking along by the wall and remembered that the dog was in the cellar. Full of remorse he hurried to him with handfuls of food, only to find Silver too weak to eat. But somehow he managed to save him and the dog gulped down the food, wagging his tail and looking at Jamie as he did in real life.

Jamie's grief and fear were so real that he woke in terror, trembling in the shadowy bedroom, relieved to find himself in bed. It was to become a regular dream with Jamie until one day he dreamed that it was too late. He found Silver dead and he woke up crying real tears.

III

Jamie tried to get a job as a newspaper boy. He saw the position offered as he passed a newsagent's on the way to school—BOY WANTED TO DELIVER EVENING PAPERS ran the notice in the window, and Jamie eagerly applied.

The newsagent was a little man with big glasses. He peered through them doubtfully at Jamie, taking in his small stature and thinness.

"How old are you?" was the first question.

"Eleven."

"Too young," retorted the newsagent. "Far too young."

Jamie stared at him, not realizing that the interview was at an end.

"Well?" said the man when Jamie did not turn away.

"Please, mister, I need the money. I'm not too young. I'd be good at it."

"Against the law. I can't break the law," was his only explanation and Jamie had no answer to that.

He would have to find some other way of making money but so far he did not know how. But the problem of money was only the first of many that Jamie was to face.

9

Lost

Jamie's money problems became more acute because Hilliard suddenly asked for the return of his loan. He came up to Jamie in the playground one afternoon and said, "Hey, Vince, don't forget you owe me a fiver."

Jamie said nothing, not certain as to whether an answer was required, but there was a sinking feeling in his stomach as he thought of the five pounds, for he could never repay it.

"Well," continued Hilliard. "What about it?"

Jamie still hesitated, not knowing what to say. At last he replied: "I haven't got it yet, Hilliard. I told you I couldn't give it back."

"When will you, then? I didn't give you the money, kid. I only lent it to you."

"I know, Hilliard. I haven't forgotten it, honest I haven't. I've been saving my money, but it takes time. I'll give it back to you just as soon as I can. I promise."

"You'd better," retorted Hilliard menacingly. "Or else . . ."

He said no more, but left the younger boy to consider this doubtful threat, and Jamie realized that Hilliard was not so kind and friendly as he had at first seemed.

The debt and Hilliard's threat were just two more burdens to add to his troubles, although he was becoming used to them now and could lie smoothly to his mother as to his whereabouts each evening and to his sister as to his whereabouts during the lunch hour. But how hungry he always was! His mother packed him some sandwiches every day for him to eat during the morning break and for half an hour he would walk around the streets at lunchtime, munching them as he looked in shop windows, not daring to remain in the playground in case he should be seen by one of the teachers.

Cora was very suspicious. She knew that Jamie did not go to lunch but she could not prove it, while his emphatic denials to her accusations made her doubt herself. But she looked for him every day in the lunch hall and never did she see him there.

And that boy Hilliard. What had Jamie to do with him? She had seen them talking together in the playground, Jamie looking uncomfortable, Hilliard menacing, but when she questioned her brother about it he made vague replies or told her to mind her own business. Cora, like everyone else, knew of Hilliard's reputation and she was afraid for Jamie.

Ever since he had told his mother that he hated her Jamie had gradually become a different boy, surrounded by mysteries, spending long hours away from home and becoming surly and uncommunicative. Somehow Cora connected his behavior with the dog, especially as he never spoke of Silver now, but how or where the connection lay she could not decide. She kept her suspicions to herself, having nothing definite to go on, but she kept her ears well open while in school and questioned Jamie constantly, trying to find an opening, hoping to trip him up.

Jamie knew what she was up to and because he could not always remember the excuses he had made he resolved to say nothing, listening silently and with blank expression as Cora ranted and taunted, pleaded and coaxed.

"I'll tell Mum you don't go to dinners if you don't tell me where you go," she threatened one day. "Where do you go, Jamie? I know you're never in the hall. Don't you get hungry?"

"Leave me alone," was Jamie's surly reply. "It's none of your business what I do."

Cora was not deterred.

"And why do you want to go getting friendly with that Hilliard? He's no good. Everybody says so."

"What do you know about him?" said Jamie sharply.

"Same as what everybody knows. Same as what he tells us."

"What's that?"

"I'm not telling," replied Cora. "Not unless you tell me where you go at dinnertime."

"I don't go nowhere."

"Liar," was Cora's contemptuous answer. "What's happened to you, Jamie? You used to be nice to me. We used to go around together. I can keep a secret, you know I can. I've kept your secrets before."

Jamie was silent, torn with the desire to confess everything to his insistent sister and the knowledge that he could say nothing because of the lies he had already told and the trouble he would heap upon himself once the truth was revealed. It was true that he used to be nice to Cora once, he did trust her with his secrets. But now he was too worried to be nice to anyone, always thinking ahead, trying to find ways of obtaining money to feed Silver, trying to make up reasonable excuses for being out of the house every night of the week regardless of the weather.

"Oh, leave me alone, leave me alone!" he cried at last. "I'm telling you nothing."

"Then I'll find out for myself, Jamie, because I've heard things about you that I don't like."

"What things? What've you heard?" said Jamie anxiously.

"Never you mind. But Hilliard will tell me all I want to know. He told me you owe him money. Is it true?"

Jamie said nothing.

"It is true, isn't it?" demanded Cora. "Tell me, Jamie. Is it true?"

But Jamie refused to speak and by his refusal Cora knew that Hilliard had told the truth. She was determined to find out more, if not from Jamie then from Hilliard, whose main fault was that he was over-talkative. Cora wanted to help her brother, but she could not help him if she did not know what his troubles were.

II

Jamie had to let Cora into his secret. When he went to the swimming baths with his class one Tuesday morning he slipped on the wet tiles surrounding the pool and twisted his ankle. At first it was not very painful, but as the day continued his ankle began to swell until every step he took made him wince. All afternoon it throbbed and when it was time to go home he looked out for Cora, wanting her to help him.

Cora, not knowing of his accident, had dashed off with her friend, having already arranged to spend the evening with her, and Jamie had to hobble home alone, hanging on to railings where he could, feeling more and more depressed.

When he reached home his mother was full of exclamations of sympathy. She sat him on a chair, bathed his foot with cold water and, for lack of a bandage, wound one of his father's large white handkerchiefs around the swelling.

"Now," she said when she had done all this, "you must go to bed, Jamie, and rest. No going out tonight."

Jamie opened his mouth to protest, but his mother broke in before he could speak.

"No, Jamie. You're not going out tonight. You're to stay in bed and if you're not better tomorrow I'll get the doctor to have a look at you. It won't hurt you to stay in bed for once."

"But, Mum . . ."

Jamie stopped. What could he say? What reasonable excuse could he offer for going out?

"Where's Cora?" he asked instead.

"Oh, she won't be home till about eight or nine tonight. She's having tea with a friend of hers."

"Oh," said Jamie, abashed.

His mother looked at him in puzzlement, but, having

much to do, took no more notice of him after that moment.

"Keep your eye on Leah for me while I'm in the kitchen," she said to Jamie, and hurried back to her cooking.

Jamie did as he was bid, watching his baby sister crawl around the floor, examining as she went. She pulled at the chair covers, grabbed at a toy and threw it down again, and stared at Jamie with a smile. Jamie watched her almost unseeingly, thinking of Silver in the cellar, hungry, waiting for his master to come. Not even Cora could go to him.

He bit his lip with anxiety, forgetting his throbbing ankle. He would have to do something quickly, but going to Silver himself was out of the question. He would have to wait until Cora came home. But when would that be?

It was a quarter to nine when Cora came home, too late to go out again without arousing suspicion. She listened sympathetically as Jamie explained the situation in the privacy of their bedroom, exclaiming when he had finished: "Why didn't you tell me before? I would have helped you, Jamie. You know I would."

"Anyway, I've told you now and don't dare tell Mum or Dad. You promise not to tell them?"

"I promise," said Cora, "but I must say it seems a crazy idea to me keeping him in a cellar. What's it like?"

"You'll see it tomorrow. Please go early tomorrow, won't you, Cora? Poor Silver will be starving."

"Don't worry. I'll look after him. I'd like to help you

look after him. You give me the money for the food and I'll get it before I go to school."

So it was agreed and Jamie was relieved of many of his worries now that he had shared them with someone. They talked in whispers for a long time, Jamie telling Cora all about Silver, and when they fell asleep Jamie was smiling.

In the meantime Silver waited in vain.

III

Sunlight never ventured far into Silver's cellar. It was cut off completely at the front entrance and filtered almost unwillingly through the hole in the wall of the fourth cellar, so that the greyhound, until Jamie took him out, was in almost constant darkness.

He slept for much of the time, nibbling at his bones when awake, ears always alert for Jamie's footsteps. He knew when to expect him now and no longer jumped up in anticipation at other sounds which penetrated the cellar, knowing that they did not herald Jamie's advent.

There were many sounds for the old dog to listen to: the tread of footsteps overhead which sometimes echoed through the pavement to him; the occasional shouts of children; the hooting of vehicles in the street and the rumble of their passage. When he had grown accustomed to the sounds he was no longer aware of them, listening only for Jamie.

It took him longer to get used to the darkness, but it was not interminable, ending with Jamie's coming, so he accepted it. When Jamie tied him up he could no longer stretch his legs by wandering about the cellar and he often grew cold lying on the old door in the corner, dampness seeping into his bones.

On the Tuesday that Jamie did not come Silver grew impatient and anxious. He became hungry, too, and waited with pricked ears, standing on his platform, whining occasionally as every minute passed without bringing the boy. Jamie had never failed him before. He had always come at the same time every night bringing food, companionship, and relief from darkness when he lit the several candles placed in convenient spots about the cellar.

Silver could not understand why Jamie didn't come and the whines in his throat became more frequent while he waited. He licked his jaws with his long, wet tongue, for, in anticipation of the food which Jamie would bring him, he was already drooling. His eager ears caught every unaccustomed sound, and, as time went on, silence gradually overcame the streets where cars only passed in the daytime. No footsteps sounded, no children called, no Jamie came.

Silver's anxiety increased and he was no longer satisfied to stand on the old door waiting. He jumped down on to the sandy floor and began straining against the string which held him, whimpering rather than whining, almost like a puppy that has lost its mother. The strings and nail held fast and Silver wearied of pulling against it. He went back to his platform, circled two or three times, gradually pulling his legs under him, then settled down to patient expectation, falling asleep soon afterwards.

Forgetfulness in sleep did not last long and the old dog awoke even more hungry. Patience had vanished and he uttered several short, sharp barks, springing up again and lunging toward the hole in the wall which Jamie no longer blocked up now that he kept Silver tied. The constant heavy strain and jerky movements combined to loosen the nail once so firmly embedded in the wall and suddenly the tautness relaxed against Silver's collar and he found himself free.

With an eager bark of delight, Silver bounded through the hole and dashed out of the fourth cellar, trailing the string behind him. He knew exactly where he was going and did not hesitate. He cleared the area steps in several bounds and shouldered his way through the half-open gate. He turned left and running with a long, steady lope, headed toward Hyde Park, looking for Jamie.

Silver wandered for a long time around the park, no longer hurrying but trotting steadily across the grass, along the lanes, round the trees, jaws open, tongue lolling out.

A brilliant moon shone down upon the park, silhouetting the trees in its splendor. In the distance was an orange glow of the lamps in Park Lane and a low hum of traffic travelled across the flat, deserted parkland. It was a warm night and if it had not been that Silver was searching for Jamie the old dog would have enjoyed himself.

He halted every now and again and tested the breeze,

but no scent of his master ever came to him. He put his nose to the ground and snuffled in the grass. He smelled many strange scents, human and animal, but could not recognize Jamie's. He was not deterred. He had been so many times to the park that he connected it with Jamie and was certain that he would find his young master here.

Silver was conspicuous in the moonlight, appearing even whiter than in actuality, almost ghostly in form as he travelled steadily and untiringly in quest of the boy. He circled the Serpentine, stopping at its edge to lap at the water, disturbing several ducks as he did so.

They flapped away with complaining quacks and Silver watched them, ears cocked, perhaps recalling for an instant the days when he had chased a fleeing hare round the tracks of various stadiums. But those days were long past and dim in his memory. The scurrying ducks stirred him for no more than a moment and he left them in peace on the lake, gliding through silver, moonlit water complaining among themselves and quarreling.

Near Hyde Park Corner Silver left the park, no longer expecting to find Jamie there. He wandered round the streets of Knightsbridge with growing bewilderment, for he had never been in this district before and did not know his way. He hesitated often, whining softly as he looked up and down the maze of silent, deserted streets, and after a while he was no longer searching for Jamie but trying to find his way.

Bewilderment became fear, fear became panic, and with ears flattened against his head, tail between his legs, he dashed along several streets until sheer exhaustion halted him. Thirsty, he lapped at a puddle in the gutter, then sat on his haunches to rest. The moon still held sway in the starlit sky, shining above rooftops and throwing long shadows in Silver's path.

Rested a little, Silver dawdled along another street, sniffing as he went, searching for a familiar sign but finding none. He longed for his young master and loneliness overwhelmed him as hungry, tired, and lost, his constant searching led him nowhere.

He could not even find his way back to the park, straying farther and farther from home and Jamie. Eventually, exhausted, he flopped down in a shop doorway and fell asleep, whining softly all the while.

The moon could not find him in the doorway and he lay in darkness, undiscovered by the policeman on his beat and the occasional passer-by, and, although Silver's ears automatically twitched at their passing, he did not waken, for even in his sleep he knew that the footsteps were not Jamie's.

10

Found

I

Cora, unlike her brother, was of a practical nature and when she went to the cellar and found Silver missing she did not panic as he might have done, but stood and thought. She knew she had come to the right cellar, for Jamie's description of it had been graphic and she guessed that the dog, tired of waiting for his master, had gone to search for him. He could be almost anywhere in London now, perhaps even taken in by some kind person who found him wandering about the streets, and Cora realized that the best chance she would have of recovering him for her brother would be to go to the police and report Silver's loss.

It was half past eight and if she went now she would be late for school. But if she left it until after school the chances of finding Silver quickly might be lessened. Cora hated to be late for school but under the circumstances she had no choice. She thought of Jamie at home, anxious, relying upon her to care for the dog he loved so much, and she knew that she must fulfill her responsibilities to him first.

She left the cellar, dashed up the steps, and set off at a run to the nearest police station.

She knew where the station was, for one of her uncles was a policeman there. Perhaps he would be there to-day to deal with her inquiry. Supposing he mentioned it to her parents? That was a risk she would have to take, for Silver must be found and as quickly as possible. Jamie would never be happy again if he lost his dog.

Her uncle was not at the station, but behind the desk just inside the door was a bulky, gray-haired sergeant who smiled at her and asked if he could help her. Cora explained why she was there and the sergeant asked for a description.

"Well, he's a greyhound and his name's Silver. He's white in color and I think he's quite old."

"And where did you lose him?"

"Just near here. Last night."

"Mm," said the sergeant. "We haven't received notice of any greyhound being found yet, but, of course, if you only lost him last night we've plenty of time. Is he valuable?"

"I don't know. But my brother loves him very much and he's valuable to him."

"Oh, it's your brother's dog, is it?"

"That's right."

Cora smiled, confident that the sergeant could help her. He opened a book on his desk and wrote down all the particulars. Then he asked, "Have you got a license?"

"A license?" repeated Cora with surprise.

"I hope you have," said the sergeant. "You've got to have a license if you keep a dog."

Cora thought quickly.

"Well, you see, my brother's only just bought Silver. He hasn't had time to get a license yet."

"Then he'd better get one as soon as he can. You come back here this evening or tomorrow morning and I might have some news for you. And you'd better bring the license with you, so I can have a look at it. You must have a license."

"Where do you get it?"

"At the post office. Seven and sixpence. By the way, what's your name?"

"Cora Vincent."

The sergeant added it to the notes he had already made.

"And your address?"

Cora told him, adding: "And I'll come back tonight about half-past four. I do hope you'll have found him."

"We'll do our best, young lady," said the sergeant

with a smile as he closed the book. "Don't you worry about him. Someone's sure to find him."

"I hope so," replied Cora fervently. "I don't know what my brother would do if he was lost forever."

She left the police station and dashed off to school, breathing heavily and with a pain in her chest by the time she reached the doors. She excused her lateness by saying she had to look after her baby sister while her mother took Jamie to the doctor, and for the rest of the day she worried about Silver, wondering where he could be and whether anyone had found him. She remembered too that the policeman wanted to see a license and that it would cost Jamie another seven and six. Poor Jamie. Would his troubles never end?

II

It was a policeman who found Silver. He saw the old dog wandering up and down the busy streets, hesitating at the curbs, whining, halting, looking very lost as he stared up at every passer-by. When Silver sat on the pavement to rest awhile the policeman went up to him, a little wary in case the dog should fly at him, uttering coaxing sounds and saying softly: "Good boy. Here, boy. What's the matter?"

Silver pricked his flattened ears and stared at the approaching policeman. He was not sure whether he should stay or flee and he watched the blue-uniformed figure with suspicion, listening to his voice but finding no threat in it. By this time the policeman was very close, close enough to see the long string attached to

Silver's collar and to realize for certain that the grey-hound was a stray.

He whistled softly and uttered more coaxing words. Silver, lonely and bewildered, hungry and thirsty, allowed the policeman to take hold of him. He was unused to fending for himself and was glad to suddenly become someone's interest. The policeman patted him and fondled his ears, at the same time looking for an identity disk on the collar, but finding none.

"No name and address on you, my lad," he said to Silver, and the old dog in gratitude licked the hand that fondled him.

His fear died. Even though he had not found Jamie someone had come to him and someone cared.

When the policeman took hold of the string and gently pulled at it Silver gladly rose and followed. Unhurriedly they made their way to the police station, and very soon, after the constable had made a report, Silver found himself with a plate of food in front of him, sausages and mashed potatoes and sprouts from the canteen. Hungrily he gulped them down, dropping the sausages on the floor with a tiny yelp at first because they were very hot, but snatching them up again between his teeth, gingerly, eagerly, and giving great gasps as he swallowed them.

The several policemen off-duty stood in a circle around him, watching with pleasure and amusement. Silver ignored them, licking up every morsel on the plate and also the pieces which had fallen on the floor, pushing the plate aside with his nose in order to get at the awkward pieces. Then he was given a dish of water and when he was satisfied he was chained in the yard at the back of the station, a dish of water beside him, to wait until someone claimed him.

It was a warm afternoon. The sun shone down on the yard unceasingly and Silver, with a full belly, grew sleepy in its warmth. He licked his jaws and flopped on his side, very soon falling asleep. But his sleep was troubled because Jamie was not there and he whined often although he did not open his eyes.

So the afternoon passed away, the sky blue with only a few scattered, drifting clouds. A policeman came to look at the dog and reported him sleeping. Later, when he looked again, he found him awake and straining to free himself from the chain.

"What's the matter, boy? You wanting to go home? Don't worry. You will soon."

Silver stopped struggling to listen. He did not understand the words but they sounded comforting. He drank the water provided and sat down to more patient waiting, thinking of Jamie, longing for him, but knowing that he could neither escape the chain nor find Jamie himself.

He dozed again in the shadow of the wall to which he was tied and was awakened by footsteps and voices. He jumped up with a start for someone's hands were about his neck, releasing him from the chain. The hands were those of a policeman but there was a girl watching, too, a girl he did not recognize. He was taken into the station, the string tied to his collar again and put into the hands of the girl.

She said, "Come on, Silver," and the dog looked at her with expectation in his yellow eyes.

She used the sound which Jamie and the old man always used when they spoke to him. Silver. And he was eager to go with her when she led him away for he knew that somehow she was connected with Jamie.

Cora, after signing the register in receipt of the dog, took Silver back to the cellar. They walked across the park and it took them nearly an hour to reach the familiar street. Silver, once again recognizing his surroundings, was excited. He pulled against the string and looked from left to right, halting now and again, still searching for Jamie, bewildered by the strangeness of all that had happened to him lately.

He put his trust in Cora, but still there was no Jamie, even when he was back in the cellar. Cora had a parcel of food for him, a mixture of bones and bits of meat which the butcher had given her for sixpence, and a packet of dog biscuits. She had filled a milk bottle with water at school and poured this into an enamel bowl which Jamie had bought for the purpose. While Silver ate his supper, Cora looked about the cellar, trying to find a suitable place to which she could tie him.

There was nothing, but she remembered the twisted milk crate which lay among the rubble outside the cellar. She dragged it in and tied Silver to it, quite certain that he would be unable to run away again with such a weight attached to his collar. Then, knowing that her mother would wonder where she was, she gave Silver a final pat and left him, promising: "Jamie will be here tomorrow. So don't worry, Silver. Jamie'll come."

Silver listened until her footsteps had faded away and when he could no longer hear them loneliness overwhelmed him again. The meat and biscuits finished, the water drunk, he jumped up on to the old door and made himself comfortable for sleep. There was nothing else for him to do now but sleep and Silver uttered a heavy sigh as he rested his thin, white muzzle on his paws, staring into the gloom of the cellar unseeingly, his heart with Jamie who had not come to him.

III

After two days in bed Jamie's ankle was more or less better. It pained him a little now and then, but after Cora had related all that had happened to Silver he was afraid to stay away from his dog any longer. He told his mother he was better and asked to go back to school, a request she could hardly understand, for Jamie hated school, even more so these days. However, she gladly let him go, for Leah was enough to look after without having Jamie home all day too.

Silver was overjoyed when he heard the familiar footsteps hurrying toward him and greeted Jamie with a cry halfway between a bark and a yelp of delight. He fawned all over him, scrabbling at him with his legs, yelping and barking and panting with delight. Jamie laughed with pleasure at the welcome the old dog gave him and he kissed and hugged and patted him in return, saying his name over and over again.

Then he untied him and took him for a walk. They raced across the park together, Silver in the lead, turning his head now and again to make sure that Jamie followed. In the park, Jamie had his first opportunity to see how Silver could run. He had never seen the old dog run before for Silver had always preferred to stay by his side, only occasionally prancing away but rarely moving with any speed. But on this day, when Jamie came back after what seemed an age, Silver was overwhelmed with joy. The old desire to race welled up in his heart and when Jamie began to run, in spite of his ankle, Silver wanted to run too.

He stretched out his old thin legs and swept across the grass and Jamie stopped to watch him, mouth open with surprise and delight.

"Silver, Silver!" he exclaimed, and the greyhound, hearing his cry, came rushing back, head low, legs seemingly doubled under him.

He swerved round the boy and jumped up to his shoulders. His strength was enough to knock Jamie backwards and he fell with a laugh into the grass, Silver on top of him, barking and panting, long tongue dripping hot saliva all over the boy. They sat up together and Jamie was still laughing.

What did it matter about owing money to Hilliard? What did it matter about keeping Silver a secret? What did anything matter when he had such a wonderful dog, which could run so fast and which showered so much affection upon him?

Jamie remembered Silver's full name, which he had almost forgotten, for he never used it. Silver Streak. He

knew now how the greyhound came to possess such a
name, for, dashing across the bright green grass, close
to the ground, the sun shining upon him, he looked just
like a streak of silver, and Jamie's heart was filled with
pride at owning such a dog.

He went home so happy that night that his mother
wondered at the brightness of his eyes and the smile
upon his face, for so often he was moody and dull. But
she said nothing, for she liked to see Jamie happy and
she thought that perhaps at long last he had got over
his sadness when she told him he could not have a dog.

Jamie's first obligation was to buy a license for Silver
and take it to the police station. He hated having to do
this, for his store of money had dwindled exceedingly
and the seven and six cut it down to no more than a
couple of shillings. He took Silver with him to the post
office and reluctantly handed over his savings and if
Cora had not told him that she knew a good way of
making money when the holidays came he would have
been almost desperate.

There were only two weeks to the summer holidays
and Jamie looked forward to them exceedingly for several
reasons. He would have five weeks of uninterrupted
company with Silver from morning to night; he would be
able to make some money in his spare time; and he
would be able to escape Hilliard's menaces, which were
becoming a daily misery to his life.

He tried to escape Hilliard in the playground, but he
could not escape him in the classroom. Hilliard did not
always say anything, but the way he looked at Jamie

sometimes was enough to strike fear into the younger boy's heart. How he wished he had never borrowed the five pounds or, at least, never borrowed them from Hilliard, and only his love for Silver and the happiness the old dog poured into his heart gave him the courage to sit in the classroom daily, ignoring the stubs of pencil thrown at him or the little notes left in his desk to remind him of his debt.

11

Summer Holiday

I

Those five weeks during the months of July and August were the best that Jamie ever spent with Silver. There was not a single morning in all that time when he did not wake up with a smile on his face, his heart singing with joy at the prospect of another whole day with Silver. They went to the park together, they played on the bombed site, they even went farther afield by bus or tube to Epping Forest and Belmont. But this was not until Jamie and Cora started to earn money to keep Silver.

Their first idea was to collect waste paper. At that time there were advertisements everywhere urging people to save paper and Cora knew of a rag-and-bone merchant who paid three halfpence for every pound of rags or papers brought to him. Jamie, Cora, and Silver stopped at almost every door along every street, ringing and knocking, asking for papers and old magazines. Often they were successful, sometimes they were not, but after four or five hours like this they managed to make up to five shillings a day between them.

It was hard work carrying heavy bundles of papers and magazines, especially as it involved making eight or nine trips to the rag merchant each day. He was a bad-tempered old man, his shop obscure and crowded with huge sacks of waste materials and smelly bones stacked on either side of a large rusty weighing machine. He seemed to resent the children's industry, having to weigh small amounts of ten or twelve pounds so many times a day when he was used to dealing in hundredweights, and, muttering complaints, dug reluctantly into his pockets for a shilling or half a crown.

Both Cora's and Jamie's exuberance was somewhat dampened by the reception they received in the dingy shop and also by the energy expended in collecting the papers, and within a few days Jamie had an idea.

"I'm going to make a cart for us to carry the papers in," he told Cora. "There's a lot of old boxes on the bombed site and I found a couple of pram wheels there the other day. It wouldn't take me long."

"Can I help?" asked Cora eagerly.

"Okay. We'll need to buy some nails, but I think that's all. We can borrow Dad's hammer. Then we'll be able to carry a lot more than we do now."

The next morning Jamie and Cora turned over all the boxes on the bombed site before deciding which was the best. Some were broken, some were rotten, there was only one which was any good. The wood was thin, so Jamie reinforced it with strips broken from other boxes. It was quite a task to fit the wheels so that the cart would run properly, but eventually the job was done and, sitting on another box, with Silver and Cora beside him, Jamie greatly admired his handiwork.

As Jamie had prophesied, with the cart they were able to collect more and make less trips to the old merchant, and they made much more money. But within a couple of weeks they had exhausted nearly all the papers and magazines in the district and this means of earning gradually petered out.

It was only in the morning that Jamie and Cora collected papers. The afternoon Jamie kept for himself and Silver alone. He did not want Cora with him then and went off by himself with his dog to the park or to the country. He did not often go to the country for it was a long way and cost more money than he liked to part with.

Silver had to be fed, money had to be saved for the future, and Cora constantly wanted to buy comics or go to the pictures. Jamie could not insist that she give him all the money. Half of it she was entitled to and still she was not so fond of Silver that she was prepared to sacrifice everything for him.

But Jamie's worries had faded a great deal. He never thought of Hilliard, he had money to feed Silver every day, and he spent so much time with his dog that he was full of contentment and almost overflowing with happiness.

Silver was glad too. There were no more long, daily waits for his young master. No more constant darkness and silence. Jamie came every morning and stayed with him until dusk, except when he went home for lunch. He explored new places, caught the scent of squirrels and rabbits, deer and cattle, and there were some days when he was not an old dog at all but like a youngster, quivering with eagerness and delight.

He raced back and forth, tongue lolling from his jaws,

snuffling in the grass, sniffing at trees and flowers and sneezing sometimes as their scents tickled him, gamboling around Jamie, barking with impatience whenever the boy seemed to dally. The sun gleamed down on his bony body and his coat seemed to grow glossy beneath its warmth. He was no longer skinny, but firm and slim. He was no longer dull but sparkling with life.

Jamie was always laughing, and Silver seemed to be laughing with him when he opened his jaws and panted, eyes gleaming, tongue jerking with each hot breath. And when they came home together and Jamie took Silver to the cellar, tying him to the milk crate, there was no lingering, sorrowful farewell, for they were tired and satisfied, knowing that they would be together again on the morrow.

Jamie would give Silver a slap on the rump and say: "Well, cheerio, Silver, boy. See you tomorrow," cheerfully leaving him to go home to supper and to bed.

There were days when it rained and then there was no fun in going out. Silver was an old dog on such days, for he hated the rain and preferred to stay curled up in the cellar. If he had to walk with Jamie in the rain he would press close to the boy, shivering in dumb complaint, back hunched and ears flat against his skull. On the days that it rained Jamie and Cora stayed with Silver in the cellar, playing games or making the place look more comfortable and tidy. They replaced the sand or swept it smooth and sometimes they explored the other cellars, leaving Silver where he was, knowing his reluctance to venture into the rain.

When Jamie went off on his own with Silver, Cora

sometimes came to the bombed site alone. She wandered all over it and one day came across a place where the stone slabs were cracked and broken and there was fresh earth underneath. She pulled and prized the stone away until a quite large stretch of earth was bared and here she decided to plant a garden, for she was fond of flowers and one of her dreams was to have a garden of her own. Jamie always wanted a dog. Cora always wanted a garden.

With some of her money she bought plants and seeds and a little trowel to dig the earth. Silver one day scraped up all her plants and she was furious, weeping bitterly over the broken green stems and drooping blooms for which she had cared so tenderly. Jamie laughed and said it was just like a girl to cry over flowers and she angrily retorted that if she hadn't rescued Silver from the police station the dog wouldn't have been able to ruin her garden in the first place.

For a while there was anger between them, Jamie defending Silver, Cora mourning over her ruined garden, but eventually Jamie relented and offered to help his sister erect a little fence so that Silver should know the garden was private.

Cora forgot her tears, Jamie forgot his pride, and together they dug the garden again, replanted it, and fenced it in. Silver watched with curiosity and whenever he came near Jamie pushed him away and said emphatically: "No, Silver. No." He felt sure that Silver would understand, for he was an intelligent dog in Jamie's opinion, and perhaps he was right because the greyhound kept well away from Cora's garden after that.

So the days passed away, in sunshine and rain, un-

eventful but happy, and when they could no longer collect enough papers to sell to the rag-and-bone man they
had to search for another idea.

II

It was strange that Manny Silverman should be the
one to help Jamie make money to keep Silver. The two
boys had been such deadly enemies for so long that when
Jamie saw him coming along the street one afternoon
when he was on the way to the park with Silver he prepared himself for battle. Manny was artful enough to
punch at him in passing, then race off before he could
retaliate, and Jamie warily watched him. Manny, however, seemed unusually friendly.

"Hello, Vincent."

Jamie stopped but did not return the greeting, filled
with suspicion toward his old adversary. He saw how
Manny stared at Silver and pulled the dog closer to him,
this defensive action entirely unwarranted for Manny did
not seem in the least pugnacious.

"Is that your dog?" he asked, and there was admiration,
together with a certain wistfulness, in his pale blue eyes.

"Yes. So what?"

"Gosh! You're lucky. I always wanted to have a dog."

As he spoke his features expressed such honest envy
that Jamie could not doubt him. He felt a pride of
ownership surge within him. No one had ever admired
Silver before.

"My dad won't let me have one, though," continued

Manny. "He says they only muck up the house and leave their hairs everywhere. As if a few hairs mattered. What's his name?"

Jamie told him, giving him the full version, and was gratified to see that Manny was much impressed.

"I call him Silver for short," he added, and in those few moments the first of their friendship was forged and they forgot that they had been enemies at school.

"Where are you going?" asked Manny.

"To the park."

"Can I come with you? I've always wanted to go out with a dog."

Jamie consented and they traversed the busy streets together in unspoken contentment, Silver occasionally sniffing at Manny's hand which was near his nose. Later on, when they had reached the park and were strolling across the grass, Manny asked: "Can I hold him for a while? Please. I won't hurt him. Honest I won't."

Jamie was doubtful. He felt very possessive toward Silver and hated even to let Cora touch him. But he felt unusually magnanimous, flattered by Manny's envy and admiration, and could not refuse.

Reverently Manny took the string, feeling all that Jamie had once felt, his longing for a dog just as great as the other boy's had been, and just as frustrated. He had all the toys he wanted, he rode in his father's car on the weekends, he always had money in his pockets, but above anything he wanted a dog and could not have one.

Too soon Jamie took control of the string again and then let Silver run free. The two boys watched the old dog race back and forth across the emerald grass, stopping suddenly to examine a strange scent, his whole body quivering at each new discovery before rushing back to Jamie once again for a pat and a word of encouragement.

Sharing the old dog's happiness, watching him in silence, the two boys felt a common sympathy, and soon Jamie found himself confessing the truth to Manny: how Silver was a secret from his parents and how much he needed to earn money to keep him. He did not mention the debt to Hilliard. That was something he preferred not to think about and he did not want anyone to know about it.

"So you want to make some money?" said Manny when Jamie had finished.

"I've got to."

"Well, you can come with me on Saturday to Victoria if you like."

"Victoria?"

"The coach station. You wait for people to come off the coaches and then ask them if you can carry their cases down to the bus stops. Most of them say yes. I make about ten bob a day."

"Honest?" This sounded ideal to Jamie.

"Yes. It's easy. But you have to keep an eye open for the porters. They don't like it, though none of them would carry cases as far as I do."

"Do you get into trouble?" asked Jamie doubtfully.

"No. Just don't let them see you, that's all. There's plenty of people at this time, coming back from Brighton and places, and most of them are pretty generous."

Jamie thought it a wonderful idea.

On Saturday afternoon Jamie, Cora, and Silver met Manny at the bottom of the long road which leads up to Victoria Coach Station. It was a gloomy day, the sky overcast and threatening rain, but Manny was cheerful.

"People get depressed when they come back from holiday to find the weather bad and it makes them pleased to have someone carry their luggage."

Jamie did not argue the wisdom of this, admiring Manny's sharp business sense. Manny had told him to be sure to bring Silver along.

"The old dears are soppy about dogs. They'll give you more money, 'specially if you tell them you're doing it to buy his food."

Only Jamie's eagerness made him overlook the length of the road and the weight of the cases that afternoon. With Cora a faithful and uncomplaining ally, he followed Manny's example, approaching only women or lone travellers, watching for the arrival of coaches and taking on his customers' luggage with genuine will. With each trip the road seemed to grow longer. His customers were often amused by his offer and accepted only because their sympathy was aroused. Some of them refused or excused themselves by saying, "My case is far too heavy for you, sonny," but the sixpences and shillings gradually piled up and only when the lightly falling rain developed into a heavy torrent did they reluctantly decide to call it a day.

They returned to the cellar, Silver shivering and glad to curl up in the corner. He looked so miserable when he shivered, his ears flattened against his head, his tail flattened between his legs, cringing with dejection, that

Jamie felt guilty about keeping him out in the rain. In the cellar they shared out the bar of chocolate they had bought on the way home, two pieces each, including Silver, and then they shared out the money. There was three and threepence halfpenny for each of them, which Manny said wasn't bad for only two hours' work on a wet afternoon, but Jamie could not help wishing, for Silver's sake, that the whole of the nine and tenpence halfpenny was his.

After that Jamie and Silver went every morning and afternoon to Victoria, sometimes accompanied by Cora or Manny, sometimes alone. He found his customers widely varying in their generosity. One woman made him carry her heavy case right to a distant bus stop, far beyond his usual bounds, and as her bus came along found she had only threepence halfpenny to spare, although Jamie privately reckoned she could have parted with two shillings. Another woman only wanted her case carried half-way, as far as the Green Line stopping place, and she not only rewarded him with half a crown but gave him an extra shilling to buy sweets for both of them while she waited for her coach. She was generous in her praise of Silver, too, and Jamie was quite sorry to take his leave of her, infected by her cheerful smile and friendly conversation.

How weary he was at the end of each day, blisters growing hard on his palms and fingers, the muscles of his arms aching, his legs tired from the constant trek to and from the coach station, but he was contented enough with the money he earned and his new-found friendship with Manny Silverman.

They played together on the bombed site, football, cricket, hockey, with improvised bats and sticks, sometimes using a stone for a ball. Manny brought his younger sister Ruth along. She was the same age as Cora and the two girls got on well together, playing at keeping house in the cellar when they tired of the boys' rougher games. Cora sometimes brought Leah along in her push-chair, plonked her down in a safe corner, and she and Ruth took turns watching over her. The once empty bombed site resounded with children's laughter, the sharp clack of colliding sticks, the wail of a bored baby, and the occasional excited barks of a dog. No one came to molest them for all that they were trespassing on private property, and the place which had once been a set of dignified houses became a perfect playground.

They bought bottles of lemonade, chocolate, sticky buns, and Manny brought some of his personal treasures to the cellar to improve its atmosphere. A huge jigsaw puzzle to keep them occupied on rainy days; an oil lamp which he had bought with his own pocket money and which was a great improvement on the candles; comics and old books; while Ruth introduced a broken-backed chair, another rug, and several chipped cups and saucers. There was also a tea pot with a broken spout from which they poured the lemonade at Ruth's insistence, although the boys would have been quite happy to drink from the bottle, and all of them found much pleasure in their little "home from home" as Cora insisted on calling the cellar under the street.

Jamie's expeditions to Victoria came to an abrupt end one morning before the holidays were over. There was a policeman standing outside the gates of the coach station. He stared very severely at Jamie when he saw the boy hanging about, and later on, when he saw him approaching various passengers with his request, went up to him with a heavy frown and said one word.

"Hoppit."

Jamie never had the courage to go there again.

12

To Pay a Debt

I

Too soon the summer holidays were over. Five weeks earlier they had stretched before Jamie as a golden vista of days to be spent entirely with Silver. Now September had come, bringing with it the first signs of autumn. The leaves were withering on the trees in the square, curling up on their branches until they no longer had strength enough to cling there and tumbled to the pavements to be trodden on and brushed aside. Red, brown, and golden they fell, some swiftly, some slowly, eddied about by a teasing wind, and the evergreen rhododendrons looked cold and dull beside them even though they lived.

Jamie scuffled through the leaves on his way to school, his hands in his pockets, his shoulders hunched. He remembered how he had first come to notice the square, because the old man took Silver there. It had been spring then and six months had passed. The green that had come to the trees had faded once more. Autumn's searching fingers slowly unclothed them and by winter they would be naked again, their sooty black branches reaching up cold and forlorn toward gray and overcast skies.

In six months Jamie had grown to love Silver as much as any boy can love a dog, especially a lonely boy and one who kept his dog a secret. Silver had not seemed to grow any older during these six months. He had definitely grown younger, in spirit if not in age. But Silver hated the cold, damp days of autumn. Summer had made him prance with laughing eyes and lolling tongue; autumn made him cling to Jamie shivering, for his hair was very short and was hardly enough covering for some of the bitter days he must endure.

Jamie would have liked to buy him a coat. He had seen the dogs of many women clothed in tartan jackets, some of them waterproof with little leggings too. He thought they looked a bit stupid and felt sorry for the poor little dogs wearing them, for most of them had warm, thick hair and young blood running through their veins. They were plump and overfed, they needed exercise, and a chill wind, if they ever had a chance to feel it, would make them want to run and jump and so work off some of their fatness.

Silver was skinny and old. His blood ran feebly and his food was not always of the best quality. Jamie felt his coldness for him and wished he could alleviate it. But the two pounds ten he had managed to save was needed for food and to begin the repayment to Hilliard. It was too precious to spend on other things, no matter how useful. Food and the debt came first, comfort second.

With the coming of autumn Jamie was often reminded that Silver was not a young dog. He was nearly eleven years old and when the wind was icy or the rain heavy Silver looked all of his eleven years, downcast and cold. Jamie had read somewhere that for every human year dogs were supposed to age seven. That made poor Silver seventy-seven by human standards. It was almost frightening and Jamie returned Silver's mournful gaze with compassion.

Summer was gone, and with the vanishing warmth faded the new summer of Silver's life, given to him by the love of a young boy when his last years had been all winter in their bleakness.

Silver went back to his days of waiting in the cellar. Jamie went back to school. The cellar was cold and Silver had for a while forgotten how lonely and dark it was. School was wearisome and Jamie had forgotten that Hilliard would still be there.

Those five lovely weeks lingered in both their minds; in Jamie's as definite days of joy, long hours with his dog, earning money to feed him; in Silver's as a blur of contentment which made his longing for Jamie greater in his days of loneliness. Jamie hung on to them as something precious he would always remember, half fearing such days would never come again. They had become a part of Silver and because of them he adored Jamie as only a dog can adore.

II

Jamie had only been back at school for two days when on his return to the classroom after the morning break he found a badly scrawled note on his desk signed by Hilliard. It said: *When are you going to pay up?* Only that, but those few words struck a chill of involuntary fear into Jamie, for they looked as relentless as he now knew Hilliard to be.

He worried about the note throughout the following geography lesson, wondering how much of his savings he could afford to part with in order to appease Hilliard. Really he needed every shilling of his two pounds ten. That amount, large though it seemed, would only feed Silver for ten or twelve weeks, then he would be broke again and desperate to find more money.

At lunchtime, before he could put away his books and escape the classroom, he found himself surrounded by Hilliard and his friends. He sat staring up at them: Taffy the red-headed Welsh boy who was always top in arithmetic because he cheated, and Dave who, with Jamie, was about the quietest member of the class and whose association with Hilliard was difficult to comprehend.

"Well?" said Hilliard, waiting for Jamie to speak.

Hilliard was trying to perfect an American drawl. He was very fond of gangster films and was eager to copy his heroes, feeling certain that this would make him more impressive in the eyes of his acquaintances. For someone like Jamie, who had reason to fear him, his size alone, together with an aura of patient menace, was impressive enough. He hardly noticed the American intonation.

"I'm sorry, Hilliard," began Jamie timidly. "I still haven't got the money. I could let you have five bob if that'll help."

Hilliard laughed.

"D'you hear that, you guys? Five bob and he owes me five quid."

Taffy and Dave laughed obligingly.

"I think he's trying to make a fool of you, man," suggested Taffy in a singsong voice. "I wouldn't let him get away with it."

"I'm not going to. Come on, Vincent, where's the dough? You've been fooling around long enough."

Jamie was silent, staring from one to another, feeling trapped at his desk. He wished a teacher would come in to put an end to the conversation, but the classrooms were empty now. He wondered what Hilliard would do.

"Ten shillings, then," he said at last, desperately. "I'll pay you the rest when I can, bit by bit."

"No. You've had long enough."

"But I haven't got the money."

His voice came out strained. He was trying to overcome the lump in his throat, the tears which threatened to engulf him at any moment.

"Then you'll have to get it. Won't he, fellows?"

Dave and Taffy nodded.

"How?"

Hilliard smiled. He knew he had Jamie exactly where he wanted him and he enjoyed the cat-and-mouse game he played.

"Remember I told you once you could do a little job for me one day?"

Jamie nodded reluctantly. He wasn't sure that he wanted to do anything for Hilliard.

"Well, the time's come for you to keep your word. And there's money in it for you. Enough to pay me back what you lent."

Hilliard could never remember when he should use "lend" or "borrow", but Jamie did not notice his slip, his doubts increasing as the older boy outlined the "little job" he had in mind.

"All you got to do is open a window. Simple as that. A window and a door. If you do that I'll let you off half the money. Then some other time you can maybe open another window."

"What window?"

"Never mind what window. You just meet us outside school tomorrow night at eight and you'll find out. Okay?"

Jamie was silent. He knew what Hilliard wanted him to do. He too had heard the rumors that went around the school, that Hilliard was a thief, and he was terrified of being involved with him. But if he did not do it how would he ever pay off the debt? Supposing he should be caught? Supposing . . . ?

"Well, man, what do you say?" Taffy broke in upon his thoughts.

Jamie licked his lips which were suddenly dry in his nervousness.

"Okay," he said. There was nothing else he could do but agree.

For the rest of the day Jamie's mind was in a turmoil. He had already told so many untruths in order to keep Silver a secret, he had done so many bad things in his love for the dog which he would never normally have done, and guilt weighed heavily upon him. It had been bad enough borrowing the money from Hilliard, deceiving his mother from day to day, worrying all the time about feeding Silver. Now there was this new thing, which was far worse than all the rest put together.

To pay back the debt he would have to commit a crime, not only one but perhaps two or three. Then he would need more money and would perhaps have to help Hilliard in other "little jobs." Where would it end? Where would it ever end? He bit his lip and blinked his eyes to keep back the tears of desperation and he found himself trembling with the effort.

III

The street was long, dark, and silent. It was well off the main road and no sound reached the four boys except that of their own footsteps and breathing. There was only one street lamp which gave out a dingy glow from its single bulb, flinging a gaunt shadow of the lamppost across the pavement in a crooked line.

The street was little more than a lane running between the backs of warehouses, and bleak, soot-blackened walls rose up on either side of it, mingling with the darkness of the gloomy sky in which hardly a star was visible. Numerous foggy-paned windows broke the monotony of the endless bricks, windows so small that only someone as skinny as Jamie could squeeze through them, hence Hilliard's need of him. The windows were far above Jamie's head but that was no problem.

With a "Well, come on. Let's get started," Hilliard suddenly grabbed Jamie and swung him up on to his shoulders.

"You get in through that window, kid," he directed with a pointing finger. "It'll be open on the inside, so

all you've got to do is push it. Push hard. It's probably
stuck after all this time."

Standing half fearfully on Hilliard's broad shoulders,
hardly reassured by the hands gripping his ankles, Jamie
reached up for the window. He could just touch the
dirty panes with his hands and, as commanded, pushed
hard. Several pushes were required before the window
suddenly gave way under pressure and, although it was a
cold night, Jamie was sweating, both with his exertion
and with fear, for this was the first time in his life that
he had done anything really bad. He reminded himself
that he was only doing it for Silver and, thus encouraged,
called down to Hilliard that the window was open.

"Right," grunted the other boy.

Jamie, though small and thin, was no lightweight after
a while and Hilliard's shoulders were aching.

"Now get inside and don't waste time. Go down the
stairs on the right and at the bottom you'll find a door.
It's bolted but not locked. Open it and we'll be able to
get in. Then you take this blooming hound of yours and
go home."

Jamie in silence obeyed Hilliard's commands. He
wanted to partake as little as possible in the awful thing
he had been forced into and felt that by saying nothing
he was letting them know that he disapproved of their
actions. Somehow he had to find excuses for himself,
but it was not without fear and guilt that he stumbled
in the darkness down the stairs, found the door, and
opened it.

He found Hilliard, Taffy, and Dave waiting for him
outside. Taffy was holding Silver, stroking him, and for a

moment Jamie felt a little more kindly disposed toward the Welsh boy, for he seemed to have taken a liking to Silver.

"Right. Now get out, kid," commanded Hilliard, and Jamie was glad to take Silver and obey, leaving the others to do what they would in that silent, eerie warehouse, no longer wishing to be associated with them.

Silver greeted him wildly, jumping up at him and licking his hands and face as if he had been parted from his master for months instead of only for a few minutes. Jamie felt his fear and guilt fast receding as the warmth of the dog's welcome pervaded his heart. His cold hands gripped the dog hungrily and he pressed himself close to Silver, kneeling beside him in the black and silent street, and he wished that there could be nothing else in life but this—loving Silver and being loved.

13

Confession

I

November came. The days were short and the afternoons crawled into an early gloom as yellowish smog wreathed about the streets, clung to trees and bushes in the square, and slowed the traffic, causing pedestrians to strain their eyes warily before attempting to cross half-obscured roads. Sounds were distorted, people coughed, and in the classrooms of St. Saviour's the gas lamps hissed dully and steadily and occasionally popped.

The smog caused an eerie glow everywhere, an artificial twilight which seemed filled with menace and which the street lamps tried in vain to penetrate. It crept down to Silver in the cellar under the street, heavy with dampness, so that the old dog shivered and sneezed and huddled closer into his corner, unable to escape it.

On foggy evenings Jamie quarreled often with his mother. She didn't want him to go out again, she could see no reason for him to leave the house, and the little flat, which should have been cozy on such nights, was subdued by angry voices and the atmosphere of Jamie's defiance.

How often on those cold and dirty nights Jamie longed to be able to take Silver home. He hurried along the streets thinking of the warmth and brightness he had left behind; the glowing gas fire in front of which Silver could lie; the thick, patterned curtains drawn across the windows to keep out the gloom and drafts; the rugs on the floor. When he reached the cellar to find Silver cold and listless, when his hands brushed against the damp, icy walls and he shivered himself, he felt a desperation and unhappiness which could hardly be controlled.

How long ago the holidays seemed now! He remembered the sunshine and the warmth as if there would never be such things again and he began to realize the difficulty of keeping Silver in the cellar throughout the long months of winter. Surely Silver would die of cold. Supposing he were to fall ill while Jamie was at school? There would be no one to come to him until perhaps it was too late. But where else could he keep him when his mother would not have him at home? There was nowhere else and Jamie's heart sank with the weight of his misery, for he could see no way out of the difficulties he had brought upon himself.

Manny came sometimes to the cellar in the evening and one night he offered to take Silver home.

"If I tell my dad it's only for a few weeks he mightn't mind."

But Jamie shook his head, a sudden dart of jealousy making him deny this friendly offer. He could not bear to think of the other boy being happy with Silver in his home when he himself was denied that pleasure, not even for Silver's sake. But his fear for the old dog's well-being during the winter was only one more to add to all the rest.

Jamie had guessed correctly. Once he had given way to Hilliard there was no end to the demands made upon him. There was always one more "little job" he could do, whether it was talking to a night watchman at the front of a building while the others broke in at the back or slipping through windows too small for the bigger boys.

They were petty things that Hilliard stole: toys, sweets, and cigarettes. Jamie had no idea what he did with them afterwards, nor did he want to know, but with every job completed he owed less money to Hilliard, which was some small relief in the middle of all his troubles. He had hoped that when the five pounds were repaid Hilliard would let him go, demand no more of him, but he had underestimated the other boy's character.

Hilliard only laughed when he begged to be released from his bond.

"You're a useful kid to have around and you know how to keep quiet. You need us, Vincent, don't you forget that. With that hound of yours you need money to feed it. I can give you the money."

"I don't want any more money from you!" cried Jamie. "I've paid you back. Now let me go. Please."

"So you can squeal on us? Not on your life. You're staying with us, kid, or else . . ."

The unspoken threat hung heavily over Jamie. He had no idea of what Hilliard might do if he defied him, but neither did he want to provoke him and find out. He was trapped, all because he had once needed to save Silver from misery, and he kept his rendezvous with Hilliard because there was nothing else he could do.

Mrs. Vincent noticed the change in Jamie. She had been watching him closely for some time, aware that something was troubling him, but the questions she asked him were futile, for he refused to enlighten her and grew stubborn as she persisted.

She did not connect her son's secret unhappiness with Silver. The incident with the dog had almost faded from her mind. Jamie had been as gay as any boy released from school during the holidays, spending every day out of doors and often with Cora, coming home with contentment unknowingly expressed in his features. But since his return to school that contentment had vanished, he argued often with Cora, his retorts bitter and unkind, while Leah's baby efforts to entertain him were thrust aside with impatience.

While she worked, dusting, sweeping, washing, end-lessly tidying the tiny flat which by the evening would be as untidy as ever, Mrs. Vincent tried to delve into Jamie's mind, worried because she saw him pale and bad-tempered, knowing in her heart that it was more than just a reluctant return to school which was making him unhappy.

A sense of foreboding came to her sometimes as she thought over Jamie's constant excursions from the house each night and his defiance when she tried to prevent him. Sometimes his excuses seemed genuine enough—he wanted to go to play in a friend's house—but too often he had no reason and Mrs. Vincent wondered where he went. She asked Cora if she knew and Cora said no, but she looked uncomfortable as she replied and would not meet her mother's eyes, so that Mrs. Vincent knew she was not speaking the truth. She sighed heavily as she thought of Jamie and longed for the day when they would leave this miserable flat behind them as her husband hoped they might.

Mr. Vincent had written in reply to an advertisement he had seen in the evening paper. Truck drivers were wanted by a new engineering firm in Stevenage and with the job there was a house, a house big enough for three children and a dog, with a garden which would satisfy Cora's love for flowers. It was still a secret from the children, in case nothing came of it and they should be disappointed, but Mr. Vincent went to work with a beam in his eyes and hope in his heart. He wanted Jamie to have a dog. He wanted Cora to have a garden. He wanted to give his family the home he had never been able to afford.

Perhaps if Jamie had known of this secret earlier things might have turned out differently. As it was, he helped Hilliard with his petty crimes because he had no choice; he went without his dinners at school to save the daily ninepence for Silver; and by November his pale thin face and nervous temper made Mrs. Vincent suspect that something serious was wrong.

II

There came a time when Jamie could keep his secret no longer, when the strain of worry was too much for him and he yearned for someone in whom he could confide. Even while he made his mother angry with his defiance, he longed to confess the truth to her. He needed her strength to comfort him, for he no longer had enough of his own.

Matters came to a head when Hilliard wanted him to assist in the robbery of an old lady who kept a small general grocery store in a dingy back street near the school. Hilliard had somehow learned that she only took her money to the bank once a week for her sales were too small to warrant a daily visit but that, as she had been ill one weekend and afraid to venture out into the smog, she had two weeks' takings in the till, some thirty or forty pounds in all.

Jamie refused to take part in the plan. This, to him, seemed a very serious crime, far worse than anything else he had done, and also there was a far greater risk of being caught as the old lady lived above the shop and might well hear a noise. He was really scared by Hilliard's proposal, enough to tell him that he would not help.

"You'd better help, kid, or there'll be trouble," threatened Hilliard.

"No, I won't do it."

"Oh no? Look, Vincent, if you're not waiting for us after school tomorrow night you're gonna get hurt."

"You'd better do it," advised Taffy. "Hilliard don't like to be annoyed, do he, Dave?"

Dave shook his head and Jamie stared from one to another, seeing the menace in all their eyes, cringing away frightened, for he knew how helpless he was against them.

On the next morning he would not go to school. He stayed in bed, ignoring his mother's calls that breakfast was ready, too frightened by the memory of the previous day to get up.

"What's the matter, Jamie?" said Mrs. Vincent when she came impatiently into the bedroom. "You'll be late for school."

"I've got a pain," he replied.

"Where?"

"Here." He pointed vaguely to some part of his anatomy.

"Does it hurt very much?"

"Yes."

His mother stared at him, noticing his pallid cheeks and almost colorless lips, the dark shadows under his eyes.

"Please, Mum, don't make me go to school," begged

Jamie, and involuntary tears suddenly spurted to his eyes.

"All right. You stay in bed for the day and if the pain doesn't go I'll get the doctor. Cora can take a note to school. Do you want some breakfast? If so, I'll bring it in."

Jamie nodded and rubbed away the tears. Breakfast in bed was something special and for a moment the anticipation of it drove away his fears. He did justice to the cornflakes, the eggs and bacon, and the bread and marmalade which followed, forgetting his imaginary pain, and Mrs. Vincent sat on the end of his bed with Leah on her knees, watching him.

"You haven't really got a pain, have you, Jamie?" she said.

He blushed.

"Well, I did have. It's gone now . . . but it might come back," he added with a rush. "You won't make me go to school?"

Fear flashed into his eyes for a moment and Mrs. Vincent saw it.

"Why don't you want to go to school, Jamie? What's the matter?"

Jamie thought quickly.

"We've got exams today and I don't know nothing."

"You sure that's all it is? There's nothing else troubling you?"

"No."

Jamie could not return his mother's penetrating gaze. His eyes dropped and suddenly he clutched his side and groaned. "Oh . . . the pain's come back." He gave a very realistic display for his mother's benefit, and so, because she had many things to do, Mrs. Vincent said no more for the time being but put some old comics on his bed and left him alone.

At lunchtime she suggested that he was well enough to return to school.

"You know very well you've got no pain and no exams. You can't just stay away from school because you don't want to go."

Jamie begged and pleaded. He said his pain had come back, but Mrs. Vincent, searching for the truth, was adamant.

"If you haven't got a good reason for staying away you've got to go back," was her firm reply, but her voice softened as she felt and saw Jamie's genuine distress. "Won't you tell me what's the matter, Jamie? The real reason why you don't want to go."

Jamie shook his head. He didn't know what to do. If he told his mother about Hilliard he would have to tell her about Silver. She would be so angry. She might make him have Silver destroyed. His various fears upset him so much that he really did begin to feel ill. He trembled involuntarily, his head spun, and he longed to throw himself into his mother's arms. Instead he said weakly, his voice shaking, "I don't feel well."

Tears rolled down his cheeks and fell in heavy splotches on the sheet, gathering in speed until he had no control over them at all. He felt his mother's arms about his shoulders and her soothing, appealing voice made him break down completely. He clung to her, sobbing loudly, his whole body shaken by the force of his pent-up emo-

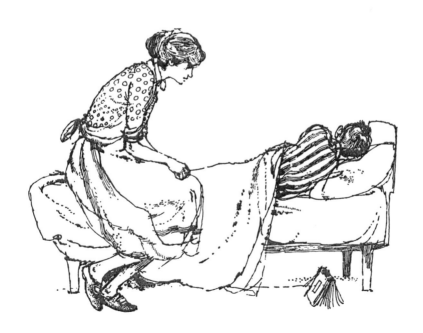

tion, and between sobs he began to let out the truth, feeling the weight of his fears receding as he spoke.

Mrs. Vincent listened in silence, except to utter an occasional coaxing word, and at first she found it difficult to comprehend his story, for it was a jumbled, uncoordinated tale. She gathered the main facts, however; that Silver still belonged to Jamie, that Jamie had owed money to Hilliard, and that now Hilliard was threatening him.

Jamie's sobs trailed off into snuffles and hiccoughs when his confession was complete. He rubbed his swollen eyes and was afraid to look up at his silent mother, wondering what her reaction would be. He himself felt better, surprisingly lighthearted, although his head ached and his eyes were sore. He surrendered himself completely to his mother and would abide by her judgment, for he could bear his worries and fears alone no longer.

"So that's what it's all about," said Mrs. Vincent eventually. "Well, well, you have got yourself into a fine mess," but there was no condemnation in her voice and Jamie took heart.

He looked up at her and smiled weakly.

"You won't make me get rid of Silver, will you?" he begged. "I love him so much."

"No, we won't get rid of Silver, but we'll have to do something. We can't leave him in that horrible cellar any longer and we can't have you being pestered by that nasty boy, either."

She got up.

"I'm going to make a cup of tea now and then we'll

think about what's best to be done. You'd like a cup of tea, wouldn't you?"

"Yes please, Mum," and all of a sudden Jamie was happy.

III

It didn't take Mrs. Vincent long to decide what to do. When she and Jamie had drunk the tea and Leah had finished her orange juice she went out to make a telephone call.

"I'm going to phone Uncle George," she told Jamie as she put on her coat. "He'll know what to do about them boys."

Uncle George was Mrs. Vincent's brother, P. C. Baxter. He was just about to go on duty when his sister telephoned and he advised her to bring Jamie around to the police station to make a statement, promising her that the matter would be looked into.

So that afternoon Jamie sat with his mother in front of the sergeant's desk, nervously twisting his fingers and biting his lip, answering questions and confessing all that he knew of Hilliard's actions, including his own reluctant part in them. The sergeant was kind and understanding. He gave Jamie a boiled sweet and told him not to be afraid.

"You've been a silly lad, but I don't expect you'll get into serious trouble, not under the circumstances," he said. "We'll see what happens." To Mrs. Vincent he added, "They'll no doubt be sending around the probation officer to have a word with him so keep him at home for a day or two."

With the ordeal at the police station over Mrs. Vincent decided to go to see Jamie's headmaster.

"You take Leah home," she said to Jamie, "and keep an eye on her. I won't be long. Then when I get home we'll decide what to do about the dog."

Jamie felt happy as he wheeled Leah along the streets in her push-chair. Everything would be all right. He could keep Silver. He need never be afraid of Hilliard again, and he hardly noticed the gloom of the afternoon, for the glow in his heart made it seem as though the sun were shining. He thought he had the most wonderful mother in the world.

Mr. Armstrong, when he heard Mrs. Vincent's story, sent for the three boys. The monitor returned to say that none of them were in school that afternoon. They had attended the morning session but no one had seen them since lunchtime. The policeman who called later at the school took their home addresses and went to see them, but none of them were at home either. No one knew where they were, but it seemed likely that Jamie's absence from school that morning had worried them. They were probably hanging about the streets.

It was almost teatime when Mrs. Vincent reached home. She told Jamie to watch Leah while she cooked the evening meal.

"After tea you can go and get Silver. You'll have to bring him home, though goodness knows where we can put him. I'll save the bits and pieces for him. I don't know what your dad'll say when he sees a greyhound in the place. He'll think he's seeing things." But her voice was light, not really scolding. She felt that Jamie had suffered enough.

Cora had not come home. She had gone to stay with a friend overnight and Jamie felt glad. He so rarely had his mother completely to himself and that afternoon she made a lot of fuss of him.

He went out happily at six o'clock to fetch Silver. The smog was thick again, muffling his footsteps, and he could hardly see more than a few yards ahead of him. There was little traffic along the back streets and the fog made him feel completely cut off from the rest of the world. He shivered suddenly. The damp air was icy and for some reason he felt oddly afraid. He had the sensation that he was being followed and he looked around every few minutes, peering through the murky darkness but seeing no one.

He increased his pace, longing to reach the cellar and hold Silver in his arms. He would light the lamp and the candles to drive away the gloom, and Jamie broke into a run in his anxiety to get there. He flung himself down the steps, almost falling, and he heard Silver's eager bark of recognition.

He called out gladly: "All right, boy. I'm coming," and he clung to Silver in the darkness of the cellar, overwhelmed with relief as he thought of taking the old dog home, away from the dampness and the loneliness.

Even while he held the dog, Silver grew tense, prickling his ears, and Jamie changed his mind about lighting the lamp, for suddenly he was afraid again.

14

Revenge

Silver was growling softly in his throat and now Jamie knew why. He could hear footsteps coming down. There were quite a number of them, unhurried but purposeful. Someone kicked at a brick lying on one of the steps and Jamie heard it plop heavily not far from the cellar. He didn't know what to do. It wasn't Manny and Ruth. They would have yelled out to him, knowing he was always there at this time of day, and Silver would not be growling.

Suddenly Silver dashed out of the cellar. Jamie opened his mouth to call him back, but changed his mind. He was scared, all alone in the darkness, especially now that the footsteps had stopped. He listened quietly, wanting to call Silver back, needing that comforting presence beside him, but he was too much afraid to move. He crouched down in the soft sand, trying to hold his breath, and then he heard a low mumble of voices.

Silver wasn't growling now. It must be someone he knew. Jamie strained his ears, trying to recognize the tones, but there were several, all talking together, and he could not tell one from another. Then he heard a yelp of pain from Silver.

Jamie jumped up, suddenly terrified for his dog, but still afraid for himself. He wanted to rush out, scream at them to leave Silver alone, but he hesitated. How many were there and what did they want? They were not friendly, that was obvious, or they would have come into the cellar by now and they wouldn't be making Silver cry out in pain.

Silver yelped again and whined slowly. Jamie heard a laugh and recognized it. It was Hilliard!

He sank back slowly to the floor again, despising himself for not going to help his dog, but petrified to stillness, wondering what Hilliard might do to him, remembering his many threats. He must know about the police and he would have his revenge.

It was very quiet for a moment or two and then Jamie heard Hilliard speak. The voice was quite plain, so he must be shouting so that Jamie could hear.

"He's in one of these cellars, I bet you. Vincent. . . . *Vincent. Vincent, can you hear me calling?*"

Jamie did not answer, although he knew that once Hilliard started to search it would be less than five minutes before he was discovered. But Silver wasn't yelping or whining now, so he must be all right. Jamie decided to stay where he was, bodily fear surmounting the anguish in his mind and his fear for Silver. Let them come and find him . . . he had a few minutes left . . . they couldn't really do anything to him, not now the police were looking for them; they'd be crazy if they did. Hilliard knew enough about courts to know that he'd never escape a severe sentence if he did any harm to Jamie.

He crawled quietly into the farthest corner of the cellar, dragging a rug after him and crouching down behind it, his back pressed against the damp brick wall. It was comforting to feel it behind him even if it was cold. They couldn't creep up on him from behind, whatever else they did.

He heard footsteps again, coming closer and louder. They were scrambling over the stones and making a noise about it, cursing when they fell. Jamie listened to their voices and came to the conclusion that Hilliard was joined by his two usual companions, Taffy and Dave. He was glad to hear Taffy's voice. The Welsh boy had always liked Silver, so he would never let Hilliard hurt him. But even so he wondered why Silver had yelped and whined. Perhaps . . .

Jamie drew in his breath sharply. Through the gap in the wall he saw a faint light wavering. It moved up and down, lighting up the sand pile, throwing shadows across the rubble, gleaming on the enamel bowl. They would be here any minute now and Jamie pulled the rug up a little higher, just peering over the top, listening to their footsteps and their panting breath.

"I know you're there, Vincent," said Hilliard. "Come on out."

Then Taffy spoke.

"Hey, Vince, we've got your dog, you know. Why don't you come out now?"

Jamie seemed to freeze. That was Taffy? Talking like that? There was such cold promise in his lilting voice. He couldn't do anything to Silver, surely not? Taffy liked Silver. Silver liked him.

At that moment a beam of flashlight shone directly into the cellar. Jamie stared at it as it gleamed down on the untidy sand, seeing imprinted upon it his own foot-steps and those of Silver. Little round pad marks every-where. He heard a shuffle and then, behind the flashlight, he saw the lower half of Hilliard's trousers. They had found him now. The suspense was over.

Still Jamie did not move. The flashlight went out for a second as Hilliard bent down to enter. It was like watch-ing an animal returning to its lair and Jamie felt trapped up in the corner behind the rug. But where was Silver? Where was his dog?

Hilliard stood up, playing the flashlight about the cellar walls, pointing it everywhere but in Jamie's corner.

"Is he there?" said Dave.

Hilliard did not answer. He suddenly switched out the flashlight and there was complete blackness. Jamie heard the other boy's heavy breathing and then he spoke. His voice was very, very quiet, full of menace.

"Oh, Vincent." He almost sang the words. "I know you're here," and, as he spoke, he flashed the full glare of the flashlight into the corner where Jamie crouched, blinding him for a moment.

Jamie stayed where he was, his hands clutching the rug as if that alone could save him from whatever harm was intended.

"'Oh, Granny, what big eyes you've got,'" quoted Hilliard, and he laughed out loud at his own joke. Then he turned back to the hole in the wall. "Okay, you guys. I've found him. He's here. All tucked up like a bug in a rug."

Dave came in next. He too had a flashlight—a powerful, glaring object which brightened the cellar and made Jamie look silly crouching behind the rug. Even a spider crawling across the sand was visible. Hilliard saw it too and stamped his foot down hard upon it. Jamie shut his eyes, feeling crushed like the spider. Taffy stayed outside.

Hilliard looked around speculatively, nodding his head and grinning.

"Not a bad little place you've got here, Vince," he said at last. "Not bad at all."

Jamie said nothing. He stared up at Hilliard and, strangely enough, felt quite calm. Dave looked nervous. He kept licking his lips and he would not look at Jamie, although the latter stared at him.

"Come on, Hilliard," said Dave urgently. "Get on with it. We ain't got all night."

"Stand up, Vincent," commanded Hilliard.

Jamie stood up, letting the rug drop at his feet.

"You squealed, didn't you? You told the cops, didn't you?"

"No," said Jamie, and to his surprise his voice was quite loud and firm.

"Liar." There was contempt in Hilliard's voice and he wasn't grinning any more. "Do you know what we do with squealers, Vincent?"

"No," said Jamie.

"We like to make 'em squeal a bit louder."

"You daren't," retorted Jamie, and suddenly he found his confidence returning.

Hilliard could do nothing to him. Hilliard would do

nothing to him. He was more afraid than Jamie. He knew the police were after him and he feared the police.

Hilliard turned to Dave. His grin had returned, which was a little disconcerting to Jamie. When Hilliard grinned like that it was because he had some plan up his sleeve.

"You know, he's right, Dave."

Dave appeared relieved, but he said nothing. He had no idea what Hilliard's intentions were, apart from the fact that he wanted to give Jamie a good scare, but he couldn't believe that he would really do the boy any harm.

There was a long silence. Hilliard stared at Jamie and Jamie returned his gaze, defiantly, almost triumphantly. Then something happened to puncture all his newfound courage. He heard Silver whine again and Taffy say, "Shut up."

"Where's my dog?" he demanded of Hilliard. "What have you done with my dog?"

Hilliard did not answer. He shone his flashlight full into Jamie's eyes again and Jamie had to look down at the floor, unable to withstand the glare. The silence continued after that quick movement and, although it was a cold night, Jamie found beads of sweat trickling down his forehead. His fear was returning, not for himself now but for Silver. Hilliard could do nothing to him, was not going to do anything to him, but what might he do to Silver?

Hilliard broke the silence.

"Taffy," he yelled. "Vincent wants to see his dog."

"Okay, man, I'm bringing him now," replied Taffy,

and he came through the hole in the wall, his right hand grabbing Silver's collar.

Silver sprang forward when he saw Jamie, a little whine of greeting in his throat. But Taffy pulled him back with a jerk and, as Silver made to snap at him, he clamped his left hand around the dog's jaws and gripped them tightly. Silver snorted and grunted, trying to shake his head and free himself. It was impossible. Taffy's hands were strong and determined.

"Oh, shut up," he said again to Silver, and the dog whined slowly in his throat as Jamie had heard him do before.

It was agony for Jamie to stand there and watch the way Taffy treated Silver. He wanted to rush forward, tear the dog away, smash Taffy's freckled face through the wall. But fear paralyzed him and he could do nothing.

"Well, Vincent," said Hilliard. "Satisfied?"

Jamie opened his mouth to speak, but there were no words. His mind was choked full of things to do, his heart beat wildly as he thought, but there was no way of knowing which would be the right thing. If he wrestled with Taffy, Silver might get hurt. If he did nothing, Silver still might get hurt. Whatever he did, Silver was in danger.

"Well?" said Hilliard again.

Jamie found his voice. It was begging, pleading, crying.

"Please, Hilliard, don't hurt my dog. Don't hurt Silver. Please, Hilliard. I'll do anything, anything you like. Please, please . . . Hilliard."

Hilliard laughed. He laughed loudly. Then he stopped suddenly.

"Get down on your knees," he commanded.

Jamie did so, willingly, hurriedly. Anything, so long as Silver was not hurt.

"Put your hands behind your back," said Hilliard.

Jamie did so, anxious, wondering. How would this nightmare end?

Hilliard stepped forward until he was right in front of the kneeling boy. Jamie looked up at him and saw a terrible expression in the older boy's eyes, a look which frightened him into speechlessness.

"I'll make you sorry you ever tried to double-cross me," said Hilliard fiercely. "Go on, beg some more. You're in the right position for it now."

Jamie could say nothing, half strangled by the huge lump in his throat as he swallowed again and again in an effort to keep back his tears. He bowed his head, not wanting Hilliard to see that he cried, and the tears dropped down on to Hilliard's muddy shoes. He became aware of his tormentor searching inside his jacket for something. His tears fell faster and it was impossible to hold back a loud sob of despair.

Hilliard laughed and then said: "Okay. That's enough. You can get up now."

But Jamie stayed where he was, crushed. Hilliard had something in his hand. He didn't know what it was. He didn't look, until he heard Silver whine again.

He raised his head, seeing Hilliard, Dave, Taffy, and the dog through a blur of tears. He felt giddy and his head was thumping with pain. He heard Dave say, "No,

Hilliard, don't do it," and Taffy retort, "Shut up."

Then he saw what Hilliard had in his hand, which was raised above his head, poised to strike. It was a wooden chair leg and, even as Jamie stared at it, it came swishing down. In that same moment Taffy let go of Silver's head, the dog sprang free, and the wood crashed down over his skull with a dull thud.

Jamie screamed. Silver collapsed soundlessly into the sand, and Dave turned pale. It was silent in the cellar, utterly silent for a moment or two. Then Hilliard said to Taffy: "Come on. Let's go."

Their feet crunched in the sand as they dodged through the hole in the wall and disappeared from view. Dave started, stared for a moment at Jamie, still kneeling in the sand, then hurriedly followed after them. When he had gone the cellar was very dark.

The sound of their footsteps faded slowly; the scrambling over the rubble again, the tramping up the steps, the clanging of the iron gate, the normal sound of shoe on pavement. Then silence. It was as if they had never been.

II

Jamie, alone in the darkness, spoke to his dog. "Silver? . . . Silver?"

He did not move from where he knelt and his hands were still clenched behind his back. He had stopped crying and the tears were dry on his face.

"Silver?"

The cellar was not quite so dark to his eyes now. The

faint light which always shone through the hole illuminated the cellar enough for the boy to see. He looked
around slowly, remembering where Hilliard had crushed
the spider, making out the scuffled footprints in the
sand.

They had been here. It was not a dream. They had
been—and gone—and they had not harmed him. But
the dog, Silver.

Oh, Silver, what have they done to you?

Jamie saw him lying in the sand, very, very still, his
eyes shut and blood trickling from one ear, the brown
one.

"Silver?" said Jamie again.

He crawled over to the dog, on hands and knees, and
looked down at him. Jamie had never seen anything
look so dead. He stared, and felt nothing.

He sat back in the sand, still looking at Silver, and he
began to think. No more walks in the park on Sunday
mornings; no more furtive visits every night to feed
him; no more worrying about where to get money to
buy his food; no more lies at home. No, that was not
quite right. There would have been no more lies anyway.
This evening he had come to take Silver home.

Never again would that old white dog run alongside
him, lick his hands, rub his muzzle gently against his
face or leg, gaze on him with those odd yellow eyes.
Silver was dead.

And now Jamie knew. His mind wasn't numb any
more. He could understand again and he knew that
Silver was dead.

There was a pain inside him, in his stomach, in his

breast, everywhere, tearing him, crushing him, pounding him, and he was glad that it was dark and he was alone. He groaned but he could not relieve the pain.

Silver, Silver . . .

Jamie was lying in the sand now beside his dog, rolling in pain, twisting, turning with nothing, nothing left. He groaned again and the cry was such that it might have come from a wounded animal, dying in its lair.

15

How It Ended

I

Mrs. Vincent waited and waited for Jamie to come home. She could not understand why he was so late because he had faithfully promised to return at once, bringing Silver with him. Now it was half-past eleven and still he had not come. What could have kept him? Where could he be?

Jamie's father came home shortly after midnight, tired and ready for bed, but he found an anxious wife awaiting him, her face lined with the strain of the last few hours, and he knew that something was wrong before she even spoke.

"Thank goodness you've come, Charlie. I'm so worried about Jamie. He hasn't come home yet. I don't know where he can be. He promised to be home early."

"Not here?" and there was consternation in Mr. Vincent's voice.

Hurriedly Mrs. Vincent related to him the events of the day, ending up, "You don't think . . . those boys?"

"No, they wouldn't do anything to him if that's what you're thinking," Mr. Vincent hastily reassured her, still astonished by all that he had heard, but at the same time there was doubt in his mind.

There was no reason for Jamie to stay out late. He had been told to bring Silver home.

"He went off so happy when I told him to bring the dog home," said Jamie's mother. "That's why I can't understand it."

"What about Cora? Would she know where he is?"

"Cora's not here. I told you yesterday. She's spending the weekend with one of her girl friends. I wish she was here. She knows where that hideout of his is. She'd be able to tell us where to look."

Suddenly an idea struck her and she gasped.

"Charlie, you don't think he could have had an accident? Those bombed sites are so dangerous and the kids are always playing about on them. He might have fallen."

"Now calm yourself, dear," said Mr. Vincent, laying his hand on her shoulder. "Don't go getting all upset before you've good reason to."

"Good reason! I think we've got very good reason to be upset. How do you know he hasn't had an accident? How do you know those boys haven't got at him? I don't like it, Charlie, and we must do something before it's too late!"

"If only Cora was here," said Jamie's father. "She might be able to help. Has that little friend of hers got a phone?"

"I expect so, but I don't know the number."

"Well, we can look it up in the book or ask the operator. If she doesn't have a phone we'll just have to go around there."

"At this time of night!" exclaimed Mrs. Vincent. "It's gone midnight."

"The only other alternative is to go to the police and I think we've had enough to do with them already, don't you? Let's try to find him ourselves first. I'll pop down to the phone box on the corner and try to find the number. What's the name?"

"Smith," said Jamie's mother helplessly. "It'll take you all night to look it up. I don't even know the initial. And it probably won't be under their name at all. It'll be under the house owner's name."

"Well, I'll phone Information. Got any pennies?"

Mrs. Vincent went to the kitchen where she kept pennies for the gas meter and handed him three.

"Be quick, Charlie. I'll have my hat and coat on in readiness for you. Just look at the time. Oh, that boy," but before she had finished speaking Jamie's father was hurrying down the stairs.

Twenty minutes later Cora, wakened by Mr. Smith, went sleepily to the telephone. She told her father what he wanted to know, describing how he should get to the cellar where Jamie had kept Silver for so long, then, bewildered and full of fears, she allowed Mr. Smith to take her back to bed. But Cora could not sleep for she was thinking too much of her brother and was very much afraid for him.

Together Jamie's parents went to look for their son, not knowing that they would find him in the cellar but having nowhere else to look for him. They were both anxious, keeping their fears from each other in an effort to make them seem less serious than they believed. Leah had been left in Mrs. Doherty's care, for Mrs. Vincent was afraid to leave her alone in the flat.

It was very cold and the smog still clung thickly about the streets. Their footsteps sounded loud and hollow as they rushed along, turning right, turning left, and the traffic lights flashed misty commands to the empty roads. Jamie's father went first down the steps when they reached the cellar, warning Mrs. Vincent to be careful because they were very slippery.

"The third cellar Cora said," he reminded her. "But you get at it through the fourth. These kids with their secret hideouts!"

He tried to make a joke of it, but failed. He nearly fell as he skidded over slippery rubble, his portly figure unused to scrambling about in the dark like this, and Mrs. Vincent switched on the flashlight she had brought, not remembering it until now.

"Here we are," said Jamie's father. "This must be it," and simultaneously they held their breath as they entered the dungeon-like place, searching for the hole in the wall, wondering if they would find Jamie and how they would find him.

They found him lying with Silver and Mrs. Vincent let out a wild cry because for a moment she thought Jamie must be dead as well as the dog. Mr. Vincent knelt down beside the prostrate figure of his son, whose arms were wrapped tightly around the dog he had loved so much, and softly called his name. He heard him breathing and sighed with relief and he took him by the shoulder and tried to waken him.

"Jamie. Wake up. You can't stay here. Jamie."

"They've killed his dog," cried Mrs. Vincent. "The brutes. They've killed his dog," and she could restrain her tears no longer.

II

Jamie contracted pneumonia. The long hours in the damp cellar, the shock of Silver's death, combined with the many months of worry and going without his meals, took its toll of him and for several days he was in a coma in the hospital, wavering between life and death. Mrs. Vincent was at his bedside constantly, sleepless and afraid, but at last the crisis passed and the doctors told her that Jamie would get well.

He was a long time in the hospital, slowly recovering, and while he lay in bed, listless and pale, Mr. Vincent received a letter from the engineering firm confirming his appointment as a driver. They were exciting days as they prepared to move to their new home, palled only by Jamie's illness, and there were few things to put in the removal van, for Mr. Vincent splashed out with his savings and bought many new pieces of furniture.

For Jamie there was a room of his own, while Cora shared another with Leah. It was a small house but big enough for the five of them after so many years in two rooms, and there were gardens both back and front, with a field at the bottom of the back garden grazed by cows. Jamie would love it. Of that they were all quite certain.

Jamie saw his parents twice a week and they told him all about the new house, not forgetting to mention the cows. Every time they visited him they expected him to say something about Silver, but he never did. The doctor advised them not to mention the dog as Jamie didn't for fear that he might be disturbed into a relapse thinking about him.

But unknown to them Jamie did think about Silver. Lying in his bed, too weak yet to join the games of the other children or even to care very much where he was, he had nothing to do but think about Silver, remembering the fun they had shared, the walks they had taken; but he remembered it all as if it had been a dream, a lovely dream and nothing more.

The ache in his heart for Silver had died away. He thought of the old white dog with love, but with love as in a distant time. He could think of him without pain, without sorrow, and he treasured his memories of Silver as something beautiful in the past. As yet he didn't want to talk about him.

III

By the time Jamie was fit enough to go home, the new house in Stevenage had already been lived in for a week. It was a long journey from London and Cora was bursting with some news for Jamie, bouncing up and down in the seat of the ambulance, eyes shining with delight. Mrs. Vincent kept passing her warning looks but Jamie was not unaware of the secret being kept between them. He asked questions about the house and his room and they eagerly answered him while Leah stared seriously at her brother and stayed silent.

"There's lots of places to play games in!" cried Cora

excitedly. "Fields and woods everywhere. And guess what. We haven't got a school to go to yet. Mum and Dad haven't fixed it up yet."

"Good," said Jamie. "I'm fed up with school. Anyway, it's nearly Christmas, so there's no point in going to school till next term, is there, Mum?"

"Well, we'll have to see about that. I don't suppose there'll be any school for you yet awhile, Jamie," replied Mrs. Vincent.

"Nor for me!" cried Cora. "It's not fair for Jamie to stay at home if I can't," she protested.

The conversation rattled on, first one speaking and then another, and Cora was excited all the time, as was her mother, although Mrs. Vincent showed her excitement in a different way. They were happy, extremely happy, and Jamie's suspicions grew as they neared the journey's end.

The ambulance stopped right outside the garden gate, and Cora, helped by the driver, eagerly jumped down, followed more slowly by her mother and Jamie. She rushed up the garden path and Jamie looked eagerly about him, seeing with pleasure his new home—the bright, orange bricks, the red roof, the white door and the wide bay windows, the garden no more than damp brown soil bordered with spiky new grass laid in squares.

"Come on in," shouted Cora. "Come and see your room. You must see your room. It's beautiful," and she dashed up the stairs.

Eagerly Jamie followed her, but more slowly, because, as yet, he was a little unsteady on his feet. He held on to the polished banister rail, his feet sinking into the new red carpet on the stairs, and found Cora on the landing, waiting outside his door.

"Well," she said. "What are you waiting for? This is it. Go on in."

Slowly, hesitatingly, unsure of what he would find on the other side of the door which would open on to his very own room, Jamie did as he was commanded. He saw his books and his model airplane, rescued from the cellar, on a small bookshelf in one corner. The cold December sun blazed in through a large, gaily curtained window opposite, and behind the door was his bed which, standing as he was in the doorway, he could not yet see.

"Well, go right in," insisted Cora. "You haven't seen everything yet."

There was a smile of contentment on Jamie's face and a warm glow in his eyes. He had never imagined anything like this. A room of his very own, sunny and bright. He went right in and looked at the bed, his eyes growing wide with astonishment, his mouth opening in a silent cry of delight as he gazed upon it.

Sprawled across the counterpane, looking up alertly as Jamie entered, was Silver. Jamie gasped. He looked at Cora and now he knew what her secret was. She was laughing with joy at her brother's face.

Silver seemed just as startled. He stared at Jamie, then suddenly scrambled up and flung himself upon him, yelping, whimpering, slobbering all over his face with a long pink tongue, his paws clawing at the boy's shoulders, his whole body squirming with delight.

Jamie could say nothing. He just held the dog tight

and let him lick his face. He couldn't believe that he was awake. Surely Silver was dead?

Cora rapidly explained for him, seeing the bewilderment in his face, the disbelief expressed in his eyes.

"Mum thought he was dead, but he wasn't at all. He was only unconscious and while she went with you in the ambulance Dad took Silver to the R.S.P.C.A. He's been in a dog's hospital for ages, just like you. We couldn't tell you before, because we weren't sure he'd recover, but now he's better. Don't you think he looks wonderful?"

Jamie did. The weeks in the animal clinic had not only nursed Silver back to health but restored much of his lost handsomeness. He had been well fed, dosed with vitamins, groomed daily, watched over by people who had made the care of dogs their profession, and Jamie was sure he was smart enough now to win a prize.

His coat was glossy and soft and the skin was loose, and the pattern of his ribs was now no more than a slight shadow on his flanks. His yellow eyes were luminous and he cocked his ears as he had seldom done before. He went wild in his greeting of Jamie and they sat on the bed together, Silver's tail beating a constant tattoo on the counterpane, Jamie not knowing whether to laugh or cry.

This was what he had wanted for so long, to have Silver always at home with him, and now what had once seemed nothing more than an impossible dream had come true.

Silver was alive, Silver was accepted by his parents, and Jamie was the happiest boy in all the world. He hugged the dog close and kissed him and Silver pushed his white muzzle into Jamie's hands, his yellow eyes gazing up with adoration into the face of the boy he loved.

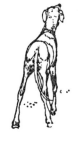

HELEN GRIFFITHS was born in London, England and began her career as an author at a very early age. Her first book was published when she was only sixteen years old, and since then she has written a number of books for young readers as well as an adult novel. As one English reviewer has noted, "This young writer knows about animals; and she writes about them as passionately as though nothing else in her life mattered. No writer can do more than that." In her role as wife, mother to two daughters, and writer, Helen Griffiths finds life demanding but exciting. She has lived in Madrid, Lausanne, and Palma de Mallorca within the last few years.

Illustrator Victor G. Ambrus is a native of Budapest, Hungary. He studied at the Hungarian Academy of Fine Arts and at the Royal College of Art in London, where he met his wife. He lives in London, and, in addition to illustrating books, he works as an art teacher.